W9-BMY-604

CABIN BOY

A Story

For
My Grandchildren
By Gramps

Averyl O. Reed

You'll enjoy this fiction of Cabin Boy duty on an 1807 cargo vessel. Learn of sail ship life, an interest to all ages, with a surprise ending.

CABIN BOY

An Adventure at Sea

A Novel

Averyl O. Reed

iUniverse, Inc.

New York Lincoln Shanghai

Cabin Boy

An Adventure at Sea

Copyright © 2006 by Averyl O. Reed

All rights reserved. No part of this book may be used or reproduced by any means, graphic, electronic, or mechanical, including photocopying, recording, taping or by any information storage retrieval system without the written permission of the publisher except in the case of brief quotations embodied in critical articles and reviews.

iUniverse books may be ordered through booksellers or by contacting:

iUniverse
2021 Pine Lake Road, Suite 100
Lincoln, NE 68512
www.iuniverse.com
1-800-Authors (1-800-288-4677)

This is a work of fiction. All of the characters, names, incidents, organizations and dialogue in this novel are either the products of the author's imagination or are used fictitiously.

ISBN-13: 978-0-595-40492-6 (pbk)
ISBN-13: 978-0-595-84861-4 (ebk)
ISBN-10: 0-595-40492-8 (pbk)
ISBN-10: 0-595-84861-3 (ebk)

Printed in the United States of America

In Memory of my wife
Marie Jordan Macgowan Reed
&
My daughter
Susan Lee Reed Mars

CHAPTER 1

▼

In the year 1807 Andy Thomas Murphy stood on the end of the Peabody Dock in Baltimore, Maryland watching a giant sailing ship come into the dock to unload a cargo of lumber she had brought from Brazil. It was mostly rosewood and mahogany from the Amazon basin to be used in making doors and furniture for the buildings of Philadelphia, Baltimore, Washington and other eastern cities.

It was expensive wood and carpenters who used it always saved the smallest scraps for making kitchen knife handles because the wood seemed to improve when the knives were washed in soap and water. Their wives always liked kitchen knives with rosewood handles. They were a status symbol.

While waiting for the ship to come up the river to the dock, Andy walked around checking the destinations of cargo, left on the dock consigned to various ports-of-call on both sides of the Atlantic and some as far away as the Philippine Islands and Australia. He found boxes and barrels with bills of laden destined to be shipped on the Java Sea to Brazil, Argentina and Trinidad. There was a large pile of lumber destined for Plymouth, England consigned to the Java Sea. He became somewhat excited as he wondered what all those foreign ports were like and if he would be the Java Sea's cabin boy when she went to those ports to unload.

Andy loved tall ships and every time one came to dock at Baltimore he would tell himself 'next year I'll be twelve and can go to sea as a cabin boy.' Andy could hardly wait for the time to pass. He just knew it would be a great adventure to serve as cabin boy on a large sailing ship. His uncle Fred was a captain on tall ships and had promised him when he was only eight-years-old he would make him cabin boy on the Java Sea at twelve, if he still wanted to go to sea.

Once the great ship was securely tied to the dock most of the sailors rushed ashore to see their families, some already waiting on the dock. Families had seen the giant ship as she came up the river with all her sails billowing in the wind. Sailors' families always knew how to tell the ship their sailor was a crewmember by the cut of her sails and how she sailed coming into port.

Andy walked down the dock so he could check the name of the ship on the bow. He hadn't paid attention when she came in because he was too interested in watching her crew maneuver her into the dock and tie her to the special pilings made just for securing big ships. Andy looked up and read, Java Sea. 'Wow,' he thought, 'that's my Uncle Fred's ship.'

Soon Uncle Fred walked down the gangway and Andy ran to greet him. Fred gave him a big hug and said, "You're getting to be a big boy, me hearty. We'll be sailing in about three weeks for another trip to Brazil. If your folks let you, would you like to be my cabin boy?"

"Oh, yeah, sure," Andy exclaimed, jumping up and down in excitement, anticipating his chance to be cabin boy for Uncle Fred on the Java Sea.

"My last cabin boy was promoted to second officer on this voyage and I am in need of a new cabin boy. I remember promising to give you a chance at it several years ago, so if you still want to go and your mother and father agree I'll give you a chance to learn the ways of the sea. By the way, how are your mother and father these days?"

"They're fine, Uncle Fred, they're fine."

"Well, Andy, there's one thing we will have to change if you become my cabin boy and we might as well get started on it right now. I will no longer be called Uncle Fred. I will be called Captain Murphy. I will still be your Uncle Fred but as a crew member on the Java Sea you will have to call me Captain Murphy like the rest of the crew does. It's a seagoing tradition to call a commanding officer Captain and use his last name as a matter of respect. Understand?"

"Yes Sir, Captain Murphy."

"Good Andy. That's a good start for the first lesson in seamanship protocol."

"You tell your mother and father I will pay them a few visits when I get back, right now I want to get home to see my family."

"There is one more thing, before I leave you for my stage ride home to Alexandria, Virginia where my family is now living. Do you know a young man here in Baltimore named James Mixon, everyone calls him Jimmy?"

"I think so. I believe he is part of the Mixon family that lives on the Annapolis Road, Captain Murphy, Sir," Andy replied in his new found sailor's language.

"If you find him, he will help you with learning things you'll need to know as a cabin boy. He was my cabin boy on the Java Sea for four years. He worked hard and learned all of the duties required of him and has earned his promotion. I am sure he has gone home by now. He is a fine young man and I am sure he will be happy to help you in any way he can."

"Gee, thank you, Uncle Fred, I mean Captain Murphy, Sir," Andy stammered. "I'm going straight home and talk to my folks about being your cabin boy when the Java Sea goes back to Brazil."

"Good-bye for now Andy," Captain Murphy said as he strode off toward Wilson's Stage Station.

Andy broke into a run as he headed home filled with excitement about the offer to be cabin boy on the Java Sea. When he ran up the steps and in the back kitchen door, he was so out of breath he could hardly talk to his mother about anything, let alone the cabin boy offer from Uncle Fred.

Once Andy got his breath back, he told his mother about Uncle Fred arriving and the offer of the cabin boy job.

"Andy, a woman doesn't know much about these cabin boy things so I suggest we wait until your father gets home and we talk about it then. He'll be home for supper in another two hours. I'm sure it can keep until then, especially if you don't sail for at least three weeks."

"Okay," Andy replied. "While I am waiting I think I will go see what I can find out about where Jimmy Mixon lives on the Annapolis Road. Do you need me now for something? I'll be home before suppertime."

"I don't need you for anything right now, so you go and check on the Mixon boy. You'll have more to talk to your father about when he comes home for supper."

Andy left on the run again to head down the Annapolis Road. He was familiar with most of the houses and some of the people who lived on the road. There were about nine families at the start of the road all living quite close to town but further out the road there was a half mile or more between houses. Andy decided to check on the near houses first and go to the far ones in the morning.

At the first three houses no one had ever heard of a Mixon family on the Annapolis Road. Andy felt a little discouraged but kept going and at the fifth house he was greeted by a young woman who wanted to know why he was looking for the Mixon's. Andy explained about the Java Sea and Jimmy Mixon. The young woman said, "I know Jimmy Mixon. I was in love with him when we were in school. He never finished grammar school before he left to become a sailor. As far as I know, he is still a sailor and his family all moved to Boston."

Feeling dejected and somewhat let down in his anticipation, Andy headed home. He had not walked more than a few hundred yards when he came upon a young man sitting beside the road with a packed sea bag leaning against a tree. As Andy drew close, the young man asked, "Hey, Kid, where can a man get a night's lodging without walking all over Baltimore?"

Andy replied, "I guess the closest place is the old boarding house on Commercial Street. It's kind of run down and not many people stay there anymore. You'd be better off going about a mile into town and staying at the Armory Hotel on Post Street across from Town Hall."

"I have another question for you," the young man said. "Is there anyone around here that does draying or hauling I could hire to take me and my sea bag to the hotel?"

"I'm not sure now, but old man Driscoll used to haul things for people with his team. He lives two houses from my house, and if you come over to my house, which is about fifty yards past that next street corner, you can ask my father about it. He'll be home in about fifteen minutes and I have to be getting home to supper."

Andy tried, but couldn't lift the heavy sea bag to his shoulder. He noticed the name stitched along the top band…James L. Mixon. "Wow. Are you Jimmy Mixon?" Andy asked.

"That's me, Kid. I'm a wandering sailor, home from the sea, only without a home. My family lived out on this Annapolis Road and when I got home I learned they had moved to Boston. Now, I have to get to Boston and find them. I'm sure they wrote and told me they were moving. I have not yet received the letter. Sometimes a sailor's mail doesn't catch up with him for two or three years," Jimmy explained.

"I was looking for you," Andy said. "Captain Murphy told me about you and said I should try to find you because he thought you would teach me some of the things I need to know to be a cabin boy on the Java Sea. He's my uncle and he is going to take me on the next voyage as cabin boy if my parents will let me go."

"Well, good for you lad, the Java Sea is a fine vessel and Captain Murphy is one of the finest Captains sailing out of Baltimore and Philadelphia. I'll be obliged to walk home with you and talk to your father about someone to haul my sea bag to the hotel. And, I think I'll take your advice and go to the Armory Hotel. I'd like a good night's sleep on my first night ashore in the past two years."

Jimmy shouldered his bag and the two of them walked together in the direction of Andy's house. Jimmy told Andy he planned to stay ashore for a while and find a nice piece of land where he could build a plantation house for the days ahead when he would no longer spend his time sailing the seven seas. He told Andy there was a nice piece of land down on the Annapolis road he would like to buy, if he could get the old Indian chief who owns it to sell it to him.

"I'd also have to arrange for a mortgage and try to find me a good woman to wed who could care for it when I am at sea." Jimmy shifted the sea bag to his other shoulder. "I guess that's going to take up most of the next year," he said.

"How old are you now?" Andy asked.

"I turned 19 last week on Thursday." Jimmy replied. "I have been able to save almost all of my earnings during the past seven years of sailing, which should be enough to buy the land, build a basic house and then I'd need a mortgage to build the barn and other outbuildings. When I go back to sea I'll be a Second Officer. From there I advance to First Officer and then Captain. In ten years time I should be able to pay off the mortgage and save enough to add to the basic house, making it a plantation house."

"Gee," Andy exclaimed. "You've got it all figured out. Wait 'til you meet my folks and my two sisters."

Andy led the way up the few steps to the kitchen door. He walked in and introduced Jimmy to his mother who was in the middle of getting supper ready and acted embarrassed to be caught in her old calico dress, in a messy kitchen, as she prepared the meal for her family of five. She told Jimmy she was pleased to meet him and instructed Andy to take him into the parlor to wait for father to come home. "I don't know why he is late tonight," she said.

As Andy turned and headed for the parlor, Jimmy said, "Mrs. Murphy, I am an old hand at working in the kitchen from four years of cabin boy duty on the Java Sea. If you will let me I'd be most happy to help by cleaning up behind you as you do your cooking. It's always nice to have an extra hand keeping things picked up when you are working hard to prepare a big meal."

"That's very kind of you Mr. Mixon, but I have never had the luxury of an extra set of hands when I am cooking, especially on days when my husband works and the girls are in school. They wait at school and walk home with him. We feel it is safer that way."

"Please then, let me help and it will lighten the load for you."

Jimmy walked over to the sink and started cleaning and organizing the cooking dishes in preparation for washing them. As in most kitchens when a big meal is being prepared, there are plenty of pots, pans and other dishes to be cleaned, after being used to mix various spices, as flavorings in larger kettles where the meat and vegetables will be cooked.

Andy came back into the kitchen and said, "Hey, Jimmy, why didn't you come into the parlor?" Before Jimmy had time to answer, Andy kept the questions coming by asking, "What are you doing? That's girls' work."

Jimmy told him in a firm voice, "Andy, if you are going to be a cabin boy, you need to know there are no moms, no sisters, only men and boys on a ship. They do the cooking, the cleaning, the laundry and all the other things that mothers do at home. You should get in here and help your mother and mark it down as experience toward being a cabin boy, if that's really what you want to do."

"Gee, gosh, I don't know if I want to do girls' work just to go to sea," Andy said in a dejected tone of voice.

"I'll tell you something, Kid," Jimmy told him, "You can be a man and still do what you call girls' work if you go to sea. Every man on a ship knows how to cook, sew, clean up messes and spills, wash decks and do his own laundry. At sea, it's a man's job, not a girl's job. Even if you wait until you're 16, and get an apprentice seaman slot, you'll still do the ships work, which includes all the things I mentioned, and more."

"I guess I just didn't think about there not being any women to do some things on a ship." Andy said.

"Well, you better give it some thought before you are so far out you can't swim back and no one will listen to your cries to be put back ashore. The sea is a tough life, Andy, but it pays well once you have learned its ways and become a skilled mariner. A man could do a lot worse with his life than as a seaman," Jimmy explained.

CHAPTER 2

▼

Melinda Murphy and her daughters worked as a well disciplined team setting the dining room table and carrying the hot foods, bread, butter and condiments from the kitchen. Once everyone was seated, Daniel Murphy said the same blessing he had said at meals, beginning when he and Melinda were married twenty-two years ago, giving thanks to Almighty God for the food, asking His blessings on the family and their guest.

Melinda Murphy said, "We will give our guest the first choice of everything, before we pass things around the table for the family."

Immediately Andy interjected, "He's not a guest Ma, he's my friend."

"You hush now," Dan Murphy told him, "if your mother says he is a guest, then, he is a guest. You shouldn't be trying to correct your mother on such a trivial thing."

"Ha, ha, you and your big mouth are in trouble and you haven't even taken the first bite of your supper," Andy's younger sister Emily taunted him.

"Well," Andy told her, "He is my friend and he is going to help me become a cabin boy on the Java Sea."

"That may be a little wishful thinking Andy. If you don't really apply yourself, you won't be a cabin boy anywhere," Jimmy told him.

"Oh, I'll apply myself," Andy said, "because I really want to be a cabin boy on Uncle Fred's ship. I believe I can do it, and I will do it, even if it kills me."

"I hope it does," Emily shot at him.

"Whoa, there," said Dan Murphy. "We'll have no more talk like that around this supper table. What will our guest think of us with you two shooting barbs back and forth like you never had teachings about brotherly love, especially with us living close to Philadelphia?"

"Thank you dear," Melinda said. "These children need a father's guidance once in a while. They get carried away bickering over silly things."

The oldest daughter Maria spoke up, reminding her younger brother and sister the reason she no longer joined in their arguments was because she felt it was her duty, as the oldest child, to keep the peace and set a good example for them. "I want to join in at times," she said. "I have come to realize it is useless, when I would rather be friends with you both. I love both of you."

The two younger ones held their heads down for a few moments. Then Andy said, "Sis, I love you too, but sometimes it is fun to argue with Emily to get her stirred up. I don't mean anything bad about it because I think she is a keen sister."

"What, may I ask, is a keen sister? A mother needs to know these things," Melinda said.

"It means she is the best, like the finest knife with a keen edge on its blade," Andy replied.

"I'll have to be careful I don't get cut on that one," Emily said with a snicker.

Everyone laughed except Melinda Murphy who politely asked, "Who would like a piece of my homemade pumpkin pie for dessert?"

Everyone asked for a piece with Jimmy and the two girls asking for small pieces.

After supper, Jimmy, the Murphy parents and Andy went to the parlor to talk about possibilities for Jimmy to get to the Armory Hotel, while the girls cleaned the supper table and washed the dishes.

"We can walk over and talk to Tom Driscoll about taking you to the Armory. I'm sure he will do it in the morning. It is getting late for him to harness a team and go this evening," was Daniel Murphy's assessment of the situation.

"You can stay here tonight and go as early as Tom Driscoll will take you in the morning. After all, you earned your supper and a night's lodging by washing and scrubbing the cooking pots and pans," said Melinda.

"Anytime I can earn as good a supper as I just ate from washing a few dishes, I will show up for work with my apron already on," remarked Jimmy. "You're a good cook, Mrs. Murphy. I thank you from the bottom of my stomach," he added with a twinkle in his eye and a hearty chuckle.

Maria asked, "Should we go to Mr. Driscoll's before it gets past his bedtime?"

"I think you're right on that note," said Daniel, asking "How many are going? We at least need Jimmy because it is his sea bag needing the ride to the Armory Hotel."

"I'm going, so I can see his animals," said Maria.

"Me too," was Emily's quick addition to those going.

Everyone looked around at the others, and from the look on their faces, Daniel said, "Okay, we'll all go. Just remember not to get carried away with his animals and forget why we went to see Tom Driscoll."

The walk to the Driscoll farm was nearly a quarter of a mile. They walked along at a slow pace, chatting among themselves. It was a beautiful evening with a nice breeze coming up the bay keeping the temperature and freshness of the sea air very comfortable, making everyone happy to be out for a walk. The smell of wild flowers and cultivated gardens was in the air, along with that ever present odor of freshly plowed soil, so common in the farming areas of Maryland.

There are different smells on land, compared to a lack of many odors at sea. Salt air has a smell of its own, changing only with the areas of the ocean a ship is sailing. The northern oceans have a different smell than southern oceans. There are places you can smell land before you can see it on the horizon. Sailors are said to get salt air in their blood, making them enjoy their lives at sea.

As they walked up the Driscoll driveway, Tom Driscoll came out his front door and said, "My goodness, my goodness, if it isn't Dan and Melinda Murphy with their children coming to call. What brings you here tonight, Dan?"

Before Dan had a chance to answer, Priscilla Driscoll invited the womenfolk to, "Come on the porch and talk. We can have a glass of tea. The men can talk in the barn."

"You know something, Dan we've been neighbors for at least twenty years. With all the work involved, with animals and freighting, we haven't had a lot of time to socialize. I was pleased to see you and your family come up the roadway tonight and thought we should have more time to be neighborly."

"You're right Tom. The womenfolk have had a lot more time to get acquainted than we have during those same years. Even tonight I am here to ask a favor to help out a young seaman from my half-brother's ship the Java Sea. She came in today and is going out in about three weeks. This is Jimmy Mixon and he needs his heavy sea bag hauled to the Armory Hotel. Can you do that for him tomorrow?"

"I'm afraid I can't do it tomorrow. My son went to Philadelphia to bring back a load of lumber for Robinson's Lumber Yard and I have to leave early in the morning to go to Dover for a load of hay and grain for Smith's oxen."

Turning to Jimmy, Tom asked, "Are you related to the Mixon family on the Annapolis Road, where it turns along the river?"

"Yes Sir," Jimmy replied and added, "They don't live there now. They moved to Boston and I am sure they sent me a letter to tell me their new address but it hasn't caught up with me. My father is a shipwright and he got a job in a Boston shipyard, I was told by someone who knew him as I walked out the Annapolis Road today. The Murphys have rescued me at this point, but I must get to Boston to find my family as soon as possible."

"I wish I could help you and certainly would if I wasn't already hired to go to Dover for Smith's grain. You said your father was a shipwright. He repaired a couple of my wagons and did an excellent job. I would recommend him to repair anyone's wagons. Let's walk over and see if we can get a glass of that tea from the womenfolk."

Walking back to the house, Tom said, "I got it. Yes sir, I think I got it. Jimmy, tomorrow morning about 9 o'clock you take your sea bag and stand on the corner of the Pumpkin Road. Ezra Shibbles is going to town for supplies. He wanted me to do it and when I couldn't he said he would go get part of a load and have me bring out the rest whenever I could. Ezra is a good man. I'm sure he will do you the favor of a ride into town. Tell him I recommended him to you."

"Oh, wow. Thank you, Mr. Driscoll. I'll sure do that."

Returning from the Driscoll house, Jimmy and Maria lingered behind the others a few feet. They were talking about Jimmy's plans to build a home on the Annapolis Road. "What will you do if the old Indian Chief won't sell you the land you want?" Maria asked.

"There's plenty of other land in the area and I'm sure I can find some acreage somewhere to make a good farm," Jimmy replied.

"There are new people moving into this area all the time," Maria pointed out. "Mr. Driscoll is getting older all the time and he will be slowing down or giving up his teamster and hauling work. With your experience as a sailor doing rigging, I would think there should be opportunities to get started in that line of work. You wouldn't need to spend many years at sea where it is so dangerous."

"That is probably worth looking into. I will give it some consideration when I get back from Boston. I'll talk to Mr. Driscoll and find out the cost of buying horses and wagons. I like your idea."

Daniel and Andy came in from the barn, followed by Emily who was covered with hay particles. While Daniel and Andy fed the animals, Emily played in the hayloft. Immediately, Melinda Murphy said, "Emily, you go outside on the lawn or roadway and brush off all the hay chaff you have on your clothes and in your hair. You do a good job of it, too."

It was bedtime, and with Jimmy anticipating an early rising for his trip to Boston, he was happy when Daniel said, "I think it is bedtime, everybody."

CHAPTER 3

▼

Jimmy awakened suddenly, with a start. He was puzzled. There was no movement of the ship, no squeaking of rigging, no heavy boots walking on the deck above. Just as suddenly he realized he was ashore and had slept in a bed for the first time in many months. Realizing he was a guest in the Murphy house he remained quiet, listening for some sound of others being up and about this early in the morning. His first hint of other life in the house came when Melinda Murphy dropped a cast iron frying pan on the stovetop as she was transferring it from the drain board to start cooking the morning breakfast of bacon, eggs and fried potatoes. He then heard her speak to someone but couldn't hear what was said. He decided he would get up and join them, knowing he had a busy day ahead.

When Jimmy got to the kitchen, Melinda was alone. He greeted her with a hearty "Good Morning, Mrs. Murphy."

Her reply came from a smiling face as she acknowledged his greeting and asked if he had slept well? To which, he replied he slept so good he awoke not knowing why the ship wasn't rocking. "This is my first night's sleep in a house, for at least eighteen months and I can tell you it is a good feeling."

The back door opened and Daniel walked in carrying the morning milk. He had taken off his barn boots with the aid of a bootjack and was walking in his stocking feet. He still wore the red and black plaid jacket over the overalls he always wore for milking. His face was slightly flushed from the cool morning air. He set the milk on a table by the door and walked over to the stove where Melinda was cooking and gave her a kiss on the cheek, saying, "Good Morning, Mrs. Murphy." She said, "And, a Good Morning to you too, Mr. Murphy."

About the same time the cellar door opened and Maria came into the kitchen with her apron caught up to carry some potatoes. She saw Jimmy and said, "Good Morning, Jimmy," in her most melodic voice. In nearly the same breath she asked her mother if she wanted her to peel the potatoes or put the milk away first?

Melinda said, "You better put the milk away first, Jimmy can volunteer to peel the potatoes. I don't think he will mind doing a little work for his breakfast. He seemed to enjoy working in the kitchen at suppertime last evening."

"I'd be happy to help out, but I should really pay you folks for the food and sleeping room I have had already. You've really been kind and considerate to me when I was pretty much stranded, yesterday. I sure thank you Mrs. Murphy for all you've done to help me get on the road to Boston. Someday, I may be able to do you a big favor, too."

Time moved very quickly to Maria as the breakfast hour passed and Jimmy helped her clean up the kitchen while they both enjoyed some friendly conversation. They seemed to enjoy talking to each other and Maria realized it was the first time she had feelings of wanting to be near a certain man all the time. She didn't quite understand it but Jimmy was beginning to be something special to her. She decided she would have to talk to her mother about it after Jimmy left for Boston in another hour or two.

As the clock drew near the appointed time for Jimmy to go over to the Pumpkin Road to wait for Ezra Shibbles, he again thanked Melinda Murphy and Maria for all they had done to make his stay pleasant. "I very much enjoyed being with your family," he said.

"Mother," Maria said. "If you don't need me for a while I think I'll walk over to the Pumpkin Road and talk with Jimmy while he waits for Ezra."

"That's all right as long as you work hard enough when you get back to make sure we have the corn hoed and the weekly wash finished. The kids can help you when the sleepyheads get up. In fact, I'll have them up and ready to help when you get back."

With that, Maria went bounding out the front door and ran to catch up with Jimmy, explaining she thought he might like someone to keep him company while he waited on the Pumpkin Road for a ride from Ezra Shibbles. She said, "I didn't want you to be lonely waiting all by yourself."

"Well now, that is very considerate of you. In fact, I find you are a very considerate person from a very considerate family. Serving under your uncle, Captain Murphy, I learned he was a considerate ship's captain and now that I have met so many of his family here in Maryland, I can see they all have the same attitudes and personalities. I like it."

"My grandfather on my mother's side was a country preacher who knew the Bible from cover to cover and back again as grandma used to say. He kept everyone in line and when mother married into the Murphy family, he converted all of them into being real Bible believers, too," Maria informed him.

"Thanks for the family history. I like it. A family needs to have its roots into something and there is no better place than the Bible and its teachings, especially about Jesus, the Lord and Master of all. You've got a good family and roots behind you there, Lady Bug, hang onto it."

"Why did you call me Lady Bug?" Maria asked.

"I don't know. It just popped out. I guess it was because I think you're cute like a lady bug. I didn't mean anything offensive by it. Will you forgive my slip of the tongue?"

"When I was a little girl my grandmother Murphy called me Lady Bug and no one called me that after she died ten years ago. I like it because it was my first and best nickname. I guess I should thank you for reminding me of her and bringing back some pleasant memories."

"It was my grandmother's nickname for me and I always thought it would only be hers, but I liked the way you said it, so if you want to use it as a nickname for me, I'll like it every time you say it."

"Thank you. From this day forward I nickname you Lady Bug Murphy. Will you be my lady bug when I get back from Boston and help me get my land purchase organized?"

"I'll be happy to help whenever I can, but I still have to be at school every day."

"Say, at seventeen, what grade are you in," Jimmy asked?

"Fifth," she replied.

He looked surprised and asked, "Fifth?"

"I am the teacher," she told him and both broke into a hearty laugh.

When the laughter quieted, Jimmy said, "I'm not surprised you are a teacher. You have the attitude of someone who is a teacher. From what I have seen of you, yesterday and today, it seems like you enjoy telling about things and are well educated on all the subjects you explain. I found it interesting when you were explaining sections of a flower to Emily last night as we walked home from the Driscoll house. You did a nice job and I knew you enjoyed telling her all about the flower. I learned from it too."

"Yes, I do enjoy teaching, and Emily learns better when we are at home than she does in school. There are no distractions at home. At school she is always trying to see what the other children are doing. She doesn't want to miss anything at school, but at home those others are not there to interfere with her concentration on a subject. A lot of children learn better at home."

"I think I have learned more working on the Java Sea than when I went to school. There are a lot of nice men on the ship who are always willing to help a younger man learn the things he needs to know to be a sailor. School was good up to a certain point. If I had been interested in medicine or teaching I can see where more book learning would be important. My interest was in ships and crafts. The best teachers of those things are the men who work them."

"He's coming," Maria interjected.

"Who is coming?" asked Jimmy.

"Ezra Shibbles," Maria replied.

"How do you know? I don't see anything on the road."

"I heard the tinkle of his little bell. He ties it on the collar of his horse so it tinkles when he walks. Don't you hear it? You have to listen real hard."

"I don't hear anything."

"You watch up the road and he will be coming around the turn real soon now."

Maria was right. Ezra Shibbles and his beautiful Morgan horse rounded the turn in the road within a few seconds of Maria's declaring, 'He's coming.' And, sure enough there was the little bell hanging right under the horse's throat on the collar as Maria had said it would be. Jimmy began to hear the bell now.

"I can hear the bell now," he told her.

"Your hearing must be weak if you didn't hear the bell until now," she said. "I heard it when he was about a quarter mile farther away on the road than what you did."

"I'm not surprised my hearing is weaker than yours," he replied. "At sea the wind blows hard a lot of the time and when you are working on deck or in the rigging, you can feel the pressure in your ears."

Maria stepped out to the edge of the road and waved for Ezra to stop. "Good Morning, Mr. Shibbles," she greeted him. "We have a favor to ask of you. Can you give Jimmy Mixon a ride in to the Armory Hotel with his sea bag? He's off my Uncle Fred's ship and is going to Boston."

"Boston is north of here, and the Armory is two miles south, won't you be going in the wrong direction?" Ezra Shibbles asked in a teasing sort of way to the younger couple.

Jimmy spoke up and told him he was going to make arrangements for lodging at the hotel before he left for Boston.

Ezra Shibbles looked to be about forty-five years old. He wore a stovepipe hat on his head pushed back kind of jauntily at a slight angle. With a small goatee on his chin, the hat didn't look out of place on Ezra. What did look out of place was the bright red cotton shirt he wore inside his denim overalls, topped with a bright green sweater. The hat would have been common in Europe a few years before. All the European Aristocracy were wearing them as a status symbol because they were made from beaver pelts caught by Indian trappers in the new world called United States of America. Furriers in Boston, New York and Philadelphia were shipping them to Europe as fast as they could make them. The hats were sometimes scarce because so many beaver were taken, pelts were no longer available in eastern states, forcing trappers to go as far west as the Rocky Mountains for a supply of pelts.

Jimmy climbed on the seat beside Ezra, turned toward Maria and said, "Wish you were going with me. I'll be back within a couple of weeks and we'll start on the land project I mentioned."

As the horse started moving along, Ezra said, "That little Murphy girl is a nice girl. She has been teaching my grandson and granddaughter in the fifth grade. They're twins. They like her. In fact, those Murphys are a nice family. Melinda and Maria are both Sunday school teachers at the church. Dan is a hard worker and good provider for his family. I doubt he ever misses a day of work."

"Say," Ezra said after a short quiet spell, "Are you related to the Mixons who lived on the Annapolis Road? The father was a shipwright. They moved out about eight or ten months ago and I don't know what happened to them. He worked on wagons too and did a good job repairing them."

"Yes, that's my family and he is my father. I was at sea when they moved and just learned about it when I got home yesterday. That is why I am going to Boston. I heard they moved up there because he got a good job in a big shipyard in the Quincy area."

"I'm going to be dropping you off at the Armory in about ten more minutes. I want to wish you good luck in finding your family in Boston. When you get back, if you need some part-time work this summer, I can use some extra help on my farm especially during haying and harvesting."

"I want to thank you for the offer and may take you up on it, depending on how things go with my plans for my future," Jimmy replied.

When Ezra stopped in front of the Armory, Jimmy asked, "How much do I owe you for the ride into town and transporting my sea bag, Mr. Shibbles?"

"You don't owe me anything, young man, and don't call me Mr. Shibbles where people will hear you. I'm known as Ezzy by all my friends and we should be friends after the ride we just had together."

Jumping down from the wagon, Jimmy said, "Alright, then Ezzy it'll be. I am glad to be your friend."

"Good bye and good luck," Ezzy said as he slapped the reins to get the horse moving again.

"Thank you. Good luck to you also," Jimmy replied.

Before going into the Armory, Jimmy looked up and down the street to see if other hotels might be located near where he could look for a room if the Armory turned him away. There was one door about a hundred yards away on the other side of the street with a sign hanging from one of its original two chains. It said Rooms Cheap.

Baltimore looked like all the other eastern cities of the time. It was two rows of mostly red brick buildings facing each other across a dirt street. Sprinkled between the brick fronts were several wooden buildings and occasional brick ones with wooden fronts. Most were in need of paint and repair. All looked like they had been built nearly one hundred years before. One building did stand out with its fresh paint look and larger than most size. It was named The Emporium and had windows with merchandise displayed at street level so passersby could see what was for sale inside.

It had been built adjoining the Armory.

Further down the street two buildings were being demolished. A sign in front said it would be the new home and headquarters of the Renaissance Corporation, known for rebuilding and rejuvenating central city areas of large cities. It had successfully rebuilt many European cities from the centers outward. Their presence could mean Baltimore would soon have theaters, classic hotels, gas lights, street cars, French restaurants and services common only in larger European cities.

CHAPTER 4

▼

"I still don't understand why Jimmy left without saying goodbye to me," Andy complained to his mother every day for a week after Jimmy had gone.

On the sixth day Maria heard him complaining and said, in a sweet, sing-song-like voice, "He said goodbye to me." She chuckled to tease Andy for worrying about not being said goodbye to by his new found friend Jimmy Mixon.

Adding a little fire to his brooding she told him, "Jimmy told *me* he was coming back to see *me*," placing enough emphasis on the word me to get Andy irritated even more than he had been.

Melinda Murphy had listened long enough, as her oldest daughter tried to get under the skin of her younger brother. To put a stop to it she said, in a commanding voice, "Maria, you can go out in the kitchen and help Emily finish cleaning the cooking pots. Andy, I want you to come with me."

Andy followed his mother into the sewing room, which was a small addition to a side of the room that stretched across the front of the house, referred to as the parlor. Once they had gone into the room Melinda closed the door.

"Andy, I want to talk to you about your sisters. They are having some strange feelings in their bodies right now. It's their age. They are becoming women and that's a time in a girl's life when she sometimes has difficulty with her innermost feelings. Both of the girls pick on you and tease you because you are a boy and they are unwinding their own feelings. Most all girls go through the same personality traits your sisters are having at this point in their lives. Because you are a boy, you become their scapegoat so to say. It is not they don't love you as a brother, it's because they are letting out their growing pains as they change from young girls to young women. Teasing a brother is an outlet for them. I think all brothers, with sisters the age of your sisters, have had to go through what you are going through."

"Well, I have feelings too, and I don't like to be teased all the time," Andy protested.

"Just remember what I have told you and learn to shrug off the teasing. I will have a talk with your sisters and let them know they can cause ill feelings with their brother if they continue doing it, becoming more of a pest to you and endangering future family relationships when you are adults."

"Your father and I had a good talk last night before we went to sleep. We have been praying about you becoming a cabin boy and decided last night to have a talk with your Uncle Fred about your becoming his cabin boy. If Fred can reasonably assure us you can handle the job and will be looked after by the crew, we will let you go. First we must have Fred's word you will be as safe as possible on the ship. It is not an easy thing for parents to let their son go off to sea as part of the crew on a ship, without some assurance he will be coming home safe."

"Wow, that's great. I'll be all right mom. I know I can handle it and as soon as Jimmy Mixon gets back I'll get him to teach me as much as he can before I have to go."

"Nevertheless, Andy, nothing is going to happen until your Uncle Fred convinces us you'll be coming back. Now you run along and after you hoe four rows of corn and two of potatoes, you can have the rest of the day to do whatever you want to do."

"Gee, Mom, Thanks," he said, heading for the garden, picking up a hoe from the back porch for the work she had told him to do. His mother stood in the doorway watching him walk out the garden path.

Melinda's eyes began to tear-up as she watched him walk in a strong and steady gait. She realized then, her young son was becoming as much a man as her daughters were becoming grown women. It was a proud feeling with a little sorrow blended into her thoughts. She hated to see the end of childhood for her children as she walked back to the sewing room, closed the door for privacy and let the tears run down her cheeks to ease the painful thoughts she was having.

Melinda Murphy walked into the kitchen and asked her daughters, "How much longer do you think it will take you to finish the dishwashing?"

"Hi, Mom," Emily said, "We're almost finished. I'd say about fifteen more minutes."

"For once, I find it easy to agree with Emily," Maria said, laughing at her own remark.

"As you know, your brother wants to go to sea with his Uncle Fred. He will be gone a long time. Those voyages are slow. It takes a long while to go from port to port delivering and picking up cargo. I know he is getting nervous about it. He needs some special care from all of us until the day comes he sets sail down the river and goes out of our lives for at least a year. He'll come back, grown up. The time before he goes will mean a lot to him, if we all show him we love him to help him keep up his spirits. So, please don't tease Andy anymore. He needs the love of us all at this point." Melinda turned and walked away.

The girls realized it was hard for their mother to see her young son grow up and especially hard for her to see him choose a seafaring career. They were silent, both thinking deeply about their younger brother's desires to go to sea. Their thoughts were suddenly broken when Melinda returned to the kitchen and said, "I told Andy he could have the rest of the day to do whatever he wanted after he hoed four rows of corn and two of potatoes. When he is finished there will be two rows of corn and two of potatoes still needing to be hoed. I want you girls to go out there and hoe those remaining rows. It will give you a chance to show your brother you really do love him."

"Jeepers," Emily said, "he ought to know I love him, without me showing it."

Maria and her mother both started laughing at what Emily had just said. This irritated Emily to the point she got angry with them and said, "I do love Andy, I just don't want to show it."

The laughter stopped and Melinda told Emily, "Of course dear, we know you love Andy but the context in which you said it sounded funny and we laughed. I'm sure Andy loves you, too."

Within minutes the girls finished the dish washing chore assigned to them to keep them separated from Andy while he hoed potatoes and corn to quiet his ill feelings toward his sisters for teasing him. Without further talk of Andy or the teasing problem, both girls walked out the back door toward the garden with hoes slung over their shoulders, like a couple of soldiers walking duty tours.

Andy was nearing the end of his second row of potatoes, with nice hills hoed up on both rows. He was a good worker and did a good, thorough job of all the work he did at the Murphy homestead. Both girls stopped at the far end of the row Andy was working on and talked about what they could do to ease Andy's doubts about their love. Maria suggested they take over a couple of rows assigned to Andy as a favor to him so he could have a little more time off. Emily agreed it was a good idea.

"It will be best if we wait until he is nearly done with the second row of corn to tell him we will finish all the hoeing," Maria suggested, adding "It will be a bigger surprise if we spring it on him just before he starts those last two rows."

"Yeah, we can tell him he is doing a bad job and we will take over to get the job done right," Emily said, with the same old tease in her voice.

"See, that's what Mother was talking about. We got to let up on Andy and you're saying something to tease him more. We can't do that if we want to put him at ease with us."

"I'm sorry, I wasn't thinking how it would sound," was Emily's reply.

"Well, if we're going to make peace with our brother you better start thinking from now on." The older daughter scolded.

When Andy was nearing the end of his second row of hoeing corn, the girls walked over to him and told him they would finish his last two rows so he could have more time to himself.

"What brought on this generous offer from you two?" he asked.

"We love you. You're our brother," Maria replied.

"I love you, too," Emily said. "Even though I tease you a lot of times it doesn't mean I don't love you. I really think it is because I do love you, is why I do all the teasing."

"We're going to miss you if you go to sea with Uncle Fred and we won't see you for a whole year or more," Maria added.

"I get mighty upset at you, because I have a lot of things to do and as the only boy in the family, more of the hard chores usually fall on my shoulders. When you act like you don't like me it upsets me, because, after all, I'm your brother," Andy told them.

"I think I understand and I'm sure Maria does, too," Emily said.

"Yes, I understand and we will try not to tease you as in the past. But, if you're going to take the rest of the day off you better get on your way. Emily and I can finish hoeing the garden," Maria said to him.

With that, Andy put the hoe over his shoulder and headed for the porch to put it away. That done, he went in the house to get himself a drink of water before heading down to the docks and a visit to the Java Sea. As he went in the back door his mother called out from her sewing room, "Who's there?"

"It's me." Andy replied.

"You certainly finished the hoeing in a record time," she told him.

"Not really, I got a break when the girls said they would finish the last two rows for me. They came out to the garden to do some hoeing and both were like really nice sisters. They took over part of my work." Andy explained to his mother.

"Say, Mom, can I have a piece of this left over pie before I go down to the Java Sea? I'm kind of hungry. A piece of pie will keep me until supper time."

"Why certainly, son." she replied, adding, "We think you're a good son around here and you deserve a piece of pie. Just don't take too big a piece, because I'd like your father to have a piece for his dessert after supper and the girls will probably want a piece after they finish their work."

Soon Andy announced, "Mom, I'm leaving now to go to the Java Sea."

His mother heard the door close behind him. She sat there silently for a few minutes thinking how much her son-child had grown in the past few weeks. His whole attitude had changed. He was growing into an adult faster than she wanted it to happen. There was no way she could stop it. She was not sure she would even if she could. She knew boys had to grow into men and the tick-tock of the mantle clock reminded her it was happening to Andy with every one of the passing seconds, minutes, hours, days and weeks. Tears started to well in her eyes at the thought of her little boy going to sea. Her heart filled with a silent prayer for Andy's care and safety because she knew it was more than just man who guided a vessel from port to port, loading and unloading cargo for those who lived always on the land. She knew whose power was in control of Andys' destiny and made her silent plea for the protection of her young son, her baby.

CHAPTER 5

▼

Andy arrived on the dock alongside the Java Sea walking as tall and straight as his nearly twelve-year-old body could posture. It was after he had taken about three steps up the gangway he heard a gruff voice say, "Hey, kid, you can't come aboard this ship. We don't allow visitors. Now get away, before I call the cook with his big cleaver after you and your scrawny hide."

Andy froze in his tracks and when he looked up he saw the ugliest looking sailor he had ever seen, standing at the head of the gangway with a belaying pin in one hand smacking it into the other hand which made a sharp, clacking sound. He was unshaven, wearing a misfit shirt, casually tucked into the top of oversized denim pants which hung half in and half out of a pair of well worn, calf high boots.

Glancing around, he saw his Uncle Fred in the background talking to another man he didn't recognize. He called out, "Uncle, err, Captain Murphy, Sir, this man won't let me aboard."

Captain Fred Murphy turned and seeing Andy he said to the sailor blocking Andy's path, "It's OK Silas, he's going to be my new cabin boy if all goes well. Show him around and introduce him to the cook. I want to make a real sailor out of this boy."

Once the Captain had spoken, Silas changed his threatening tone immediately. "Well now, you come along with me and I'll take you up forward to meet the ship's cook. You'll be his helper most of the time and under his wing all of the time. My name is Silas Block. I'm the Boatswain Mate and spend most of my time aloft or working in the sail locker. Whenever you have any free time you can come into the sail locker and me and the other men will teach you to sew sails that'll stand the rigors of rounding old Cape Horn itself."

"Well, Thank You, Mr. Silas Block," Andy said, "I'll sure be obliged to learn whatever you can teach me. I want my family to be proud of me. I want to be a good sailor, especially for my uncle Fred."

"What's your name, kid?" Silas asked.

"Andy Murphy," was the reply.

"Are you related to the Java Sea's Captain Murphy?" Silas wanted to know.

"My father is his half-brother," Andy said, "but I'm not supposed to act like it or expect any favors or anything. I'm just a cabin boy who is the half-nephew of the Java Sea's Captain."

"I'll warn ye right now, don't tell another living soul on this ship you're related to the captain. Sailors are a suspicious lot and if some of them learn you are the captain's nephew they'll do anything they can to get rid of you before something bad happens because of you being aboard. Just watch your back son. I think I'll talk to the captain when I get a chance and see if he'll put you ashore where you'll be safe. I just don't trust some of this crew."

Andy followed Silas into the galley and they sat on a couple of benches attached to the deck while they waited for the cook to show up. Andy learned this gruff sounding old sailor was not what his first impression had led him to believe. Silas was really a kind hearted soul who was gruff at times only to make his point and influence situations, until he could get them under control. Andy realized he was learning and this man was someone who had a lot to teach him. He was glad Silas had been his first contact with the crew of the Java Sea.

Suddenly out of nowhere appeared a giant of a man, as quietly as a shooting star sails across the heavens. "Silas Block," he yelled, "Avast there! What are ye doing with this child aboard our vessel? Why he's not even dry behind the ears yet."

Silas replied in a sharp, curt attitude by saying, "Now Jonathan Macintosh Smythe you should not get yourself all worked up before you know what is happening. This here is Andy Murphy our new cabin boy."

"Am I sure I heard you right? Did you say Andy Murphy is this child's name?" defiantly asked Smythe.

"That I did, and he's going to make a fine cabin boy. You will be the one to teach him the workings of a Java Sea man, if you think you're capable."

As these two needled each other Andy watched, wondering if they ever came to blows, or if it was for his benefit they were showing so much spirit in their adversarial relationship.

His answer came when Smythe turned to Andy and said, "All right, Andy, if you're going to be our new cabin boy the first thing you will have to learn is my name may be Jonathan Macintosh Smythe, but you will have to call me by my nickname "Mac" just like every other son of the sea does on this vessel."

Andy jumped at the chance to fit right in when he said, "Yes sir, Mr. Mac."

"That won't do. I am just the cook and the cook isn't called Sir. Remember that," Mac admonished him. "If you are going to call anyone Sir, it will be the officers. Captain Murphy is called Captain. You reply to him with a smart 'Yes, Sir, Captain Murphy.' If you remember that for today it will be good."

Mac turned his attention to Silas and asked how the deck and aloft crews were coming along getting the ship ready for sea. "Will we get out of here in two weeks as planned?"

Silas' reply was hesitant and slow in coming. "We have one set of sails made and stowed. We have to replace the rigging on both of the tall masts. The mizzen can be done a little at a time when we are in the tropics. Those two masts are rigged with snatch blocks making it easier to rig them. I would venture a guess it will take about fifteen more days to complete most of the work so we can at least head down river."

"Can I be sure of that fifteen day sailing schedule? I have to get supplies aboard and figure out a menu for the Captain's and Officers' mess. It will take at least a week to see all the Ship Chandlers in Baltimore, get supplies down here and loaded aboard. You better keep me informed on exactly when you plan to weigh anchor for sea or I'll see we get a new bo's'n mate for all future voyages. Going to sea is the most critical time in my job and I'm sure you want to eat while we're out there bobbing around among the billowy waves off Cape Hatteras."

Silas and Mac explained about the business end of getting a ship ready for sea. They told him a ship needs ropes, cables, chains, blocks, sails and canvas, along with the thread and tools for hand sewing while sail repairing at sea. There are the food stuffs for feeding a crew of sixteen to twenty men, sometimes more, if the cargo is bulk and has to be offloaded at a port without workers and cranes. It takes a lot of planning and there are hundreds of details to work out. They told him it's easy when you tell a Chandler what you need and he brings it to you at your dock.

"Andy, my boy, have ye been officially signed on? Are ye here to work or just visiting?" Mac was asking to make sure he didn't hire someone who had not signed the ship's register. "I can use you if you're signed on."

"Well, I haven't signed anything but I'll work for you until I do sign," explained Andy.

"We can't have you working without papers. What do you think, Silas?"

"The kid is going to be the new cabin boy according to Captain Murphy. The Captain told it to me when I was trying to chase Andy back down the gangplank. I imagine the Captain has to get the kid's parents to sign on for him, but I think it will be OK if he does some light chores to get acquainted with the work," Silas replied.

"That's great. I have some corn to peel the husks off and about twenty potatoes to peal for starters. When he gets that done there is dishes to wash, a couple of officers quarters to sweep, dust, make beds and straighten up any of the things they left lying around," Mac informed them.

Andy was delighted at the chance to go to work and show these two sailors a farm boy can work and do a good job even if he has never been to sea before. "What do you want me to do first?" he asked, directing his question to Mac.

"Well, let me see, now. I think it would be best if you peel the potatoes first, because that will take a little while and I have to have them ready for night chow. Come with me and I'll get you set up in the galley where you can work without being in my way while I get started on the roast beef, gravy, biscuits and desert. I'm planning to make a couple of pies if there are enough apples left in the box I bought three days ago. There are only five crew members and two officers aboard tonight. With only seven to feed, it will be an easy go."

Andy followed Mac down to the galley where he was handed a paring knife, an old apron and a big kettle to put the potatoes in after they were peeled. He was told to sit on the bench beside a low table which held the oversized kettle for the peeled potatoes.

"First you have to go up on the main deck and draw two buckets of clean water from the outboard side, where the cleanest water is when you're tied to a dock," Mac told him. "One bucket is to wash the potatoes after you peel them and the other one is for the cooking kettle."

"Are you going to cook the potatoes in water from the bay, Andy asked?

"If you are careful to bring up clear water, there is nothing wrong with salt water to use for cooking. You can conserve fresh water when you mix it half and half with salt water. You drain it off after cooking and it requires no salt for flavoring. We've been using it every time we tied the old Java Sea to a Baltimore Dock. Now, get yourself going or we won't be eating until midnight," were Mac's final words as he rushed Andy into getting on with the work.

By the time the supper meal was finished, the pots and pans all scrubbed clean and Mac informed Andy he could have the rest of the night off, Andy was too tired to go home. He found a bunk in the crew's quarters close to where Silas would be sleeping and lay down. He quickly fell asleep.

CHAPTER 6

▼

Andy was awakened with a firm shaking of his shoulders and Mac's deep voice saying, "OK sailor, it's time to get up and make the Captain's coffee. He'll be getting up in about an hour and we need to have his breakfast and wake-up coffee ready to go."

Andy half opened his eyes, groaned a little and asked, "What time is it?"

"It's time to put your feet on the deck and make like a sailor with a job to do," replied Mac. "Once we get a full crew on this ship you'll have to get up earlier than this and hit the deck on the run. There'll be no time for questions, only working."

"I was just curious. It seems kind of early to me. But, I can handle it and will be down to the galley in two shakes of a dog's tail," Andy told him.

"Now, that's the spirit you'll need if you're going to ship on the good old Java Sea with the spunky crew we'll have aboard when we leave port. This is a working ship and everybody has to hold up his end, if everything is to run smoothly like Captain Murphy wants. If one man shirks his duties, it throws the scheduled work of all other crew members right off the fantail," Mac explained.

With that Andy got washed up and headed to the galley. Much to his surprise Mac had the coffee made and Captain Murphy was sitting at the end of one of the long tables drinking from a cup as he pushed back an empty plate which obviously had been used for bacon and eggs. He reached over and picked up a slice of fried bread and after dunking it in his coffee took a large bite.

"Good Morning, Andy," Captain Murphy said. "Silas Block and Mac have been saying good things about you and they both think you will be able to handle the cabin boy position when we leave for sea in about twelve days. The crew will be coming aboard Wednesday and we will be loading cargo every day during daylight hours until we have it all aboard. Once that is finished we will head outbound on the first ebb tide. With a good ebb tide we will be able to get to open water in about ten hours. After that, if we have a good breeze and a favorable wind, we should be able to make Charleston in four days. It will be our first stop."

Silas Block walked in still rubbing a little sleep from his eyes. Before noticing Captain Murphy and Andy at the far end of the table, he let go with a big bellow for his coffee. Mac shot back at him, "Get your own, you lazy sail maker."

Just as suddenly, Silas saw Captain Murphy and Andy. All politeness he said, "Oh, Good Morning Captain Murphy, I didn't notice ye sitting there. I was just giving me best buddy a friendly blast to make sure he knew I was here for my morning cup. I hope I didn't disturb you, Captain."

"Quite the contrary Silas, I often hear your loud, thunderous voice on the Java Sea, even when I am in my quarters aft of the mizzen mast. It often reminds me of my dear departed father who was also a loud and boisterous man. Perhaps other men envy you for your capacity with a deep, thunderous voice. It may be useful some day if we have to hail another ship in a strong gale."

"Thank you, Captain. I shall be happy to be at your command if such an occasion should arise."

Captain Murphy turned his attention to Andy as Mac came over to the table with his own cup of coffee. "I want you to go home at night until the crew comes aboard on Wednesday," Captain Murphy said. "Your family has first need of your time and presence until we actually need you. It'll only be a few days and the ship will start buzzing with a crew working and making the final preparations for sea."

"I don't mind working on the ship and I want to help all I can as we get ready to go," Andy told him.

"Your family and I spent the evening together yesterday and they are naturally worried about you leaving. All they seemed able to talk about was losing you to the rigors of a sailor's life at the young age of 12 years. Your mother and oldest sister didn't talk about anything else as I recall. It looks to me as it would be comforting to all of your family to have you at home nights at least for the time being. I am sure when we leave they will understand and give you their blessings for a safe and fruitful journey."

"OK, Captain Murphy, I'll do as you say. I can always talk to them and make them understand going to sea is really my choice. It's something I've always wished for, since I was a small boy and my father took me aboard ships that were docked on the Annapolis River. I'm happy I get to go on your ship," Andy told him.

"Well, that settles that. When you are not needed at home in the daytime, you can help here on the Java Sea but will go home to be with your family at night." Looking toward Silas and Mac, Captain Murphy asked, "Does that sound like a workable idea to everyone at the table?"

Both crew members agreed it was a good idea and said they would teach him about everything they were working on during daylight hours. "I have lots of kettles, pots and pans that need to be scrubbed good with abrasives and can teach him how to do that," Mac stated.

"I don't want this boy to be just a metal polisher. I want him to learn the skills that keep a ship operating. Every day and every week he should be rotating around working with all the crew, learning to be a good sailor and officer. By the time we've finished a couple of voyages and he has a few years of experience, I want him to be as good a sailor as James Mixon turned out to be. Mr. Mixon was trained on the Java Sea. Now we have a new boy to train. I'll explain this to the crew when they come aboard in a few days. I'm depending on you two to see that my orders are carried out," Captain Murphy informed Silas and Mac.

"If the boy is willing to follow orders and apply himself to learning the skills involved with keeping a ship running well, Mac and I will be sure he works on all the different jobs, with all the men and learns as much as Jimmy Mixon learned, perhaps even more," Silas said.

"Thank you Silas. I'll hold you to what you just said and expect Andy will be a first class sailor by the time we get back from South America. Our first stop is in Charleston, South Carolina for textiles which will top off our cargo in the number one hold. From there we will make stops in Port of Spain, Trinidad; Recife, Brazil; Montevideo, Uruguay; and Buenos Aires, Argentina before heading north with stops in Rio de Janeiro and Recife, Brazil. After Recife we will make stops in Lisbon, Portugal; Plymouth, England and Nova Scotia, Canada where we will careen the ship to repair the two bow planks below the waterline. We should be back in about two years if all goes well with weather and winds. We will need some good following winds."

Captain Murphy finished drinking the last of his coffee and got up from the table, saying, "I've got to go to my office and post some bills. There are several Ship Chandlers needing payment and if I don't get it done, they'll have the sheriff after us and we won't be sailing anywhere. If anyone comes looking for me I'll be in my cabin for the rest of the day."

Andy left the ship to go home about three o'clock in the afternoon. He had several little holes and digs in his hands from the sail needles he used while helping Silas mend a couple of sky sails and three jibs. He enjoyed his day of sewing patches on sails even though his hands were sore from sticking himself with the needle on several occasions. Using a sewing palm around his thumb instead of the traditional thimble on the end of a finger took a lot of training and practice. By the end of the day he had learned to hold the needle firmly, sew with a steady, firm push until it had pierced the material, before relaxing his grip.

When Andy walked in the back door, his mother, Melinda Murphy was beginning to peel vegetables for supper. She dropped her knife in the sink and threw her arms around Andy saying, "Oh my, oh my, I'm sure glad to see you home tonight. Do you like it? What have you been doing the past two days? Look at your hands, they're all scratched and dug up. What caused that?"

Before he had a chance to answer any of his mother's fast questioning, his father came from the living room and after an affectionate hug said, "Welcome home, sailor. Your mother has been worried the ship would sail before you came home to see her again. I'll tell you, son, women, and especially mothers, take it harder than men when their children leave home. I'm not sure mothers ever get over it."

Daniel Murphy told his son he would like to have a talk with him tonight after supper and things have quieted down. He returned to the living room, leaving Andy and his mother alone in the kitchen.

Andy told his mother about his first two days aboard ship and how he had fallen asleep unexpectedly when he sat down and laid against a bedding roll on one of the bunks in the crews' sleeping area. "I didn't wake up until the next morning when Mac shook my shoulders and said it was time to get up. It was a lot earlier than I had been getting up at home."

"What time was it," she asked?

"I don't know, but the sun wasn't up, and it didn't come up for about another hour."

As he finished talking the door opened and Emily walked in with her school books bound with an old leather belt. She didn't notice Andy sitting behind the table across the room.

Melinda Murphy asked, "Where's you sister?"

"She stopped to talk with Ezra Shibbles. He was driving his team up toward the Pumpkin Road and stopped to talk. They were talking about politics in Boston and I wasn't interested in what they had to say so I came home. She should be coming through the door soon."

"Hi Emily," Andy said.

A the sound of his voice she came running toward him, threw her arms around his neck and planted a big kiss on his cheek, giving him a long firm squeeze as part of the action. "Wow, Andy's home. That's great. We missed you. How long are you going to be home?"

"I'm going to be coming home at night until we sail in about twelve days," he told her.

"Oh, that's really good. I promise I'll be good and not tease you like I always did."

"Thank You! That will be something to look forward to before I leave."

Emily walked around to the other side of Andy and after giving him another hug and kissing the opposite cheek said, "Now, isn't that proof I am going to treat you better?"

"I guess so, but I don't need all that slobbering over me. I just like being talked to in a good manner. Some of the things you teased me about kind of got under my skin and made me mad at you for a while. Just don't plant so many kisses on me."

"What's wrong with a sister giving her brother a kiss on the cheek to remind him she likes him for her brother, Emily asked?

"There's nothing wrong, only I don't want so much of it," Andy replied?

The conversation ended as the back door opened and Maria came in carrying a load of schoolbooks. She saw Andy the moment she came through the door and asked, "How long will you be home?"

I'll be home every evening for about the next twelve days, until the Java Sea sails," he replied. "Why do you ask?"

"I need a favor and you are the one who can help me better than anyone else I know of right now. I'd ask Jimmy but I don't know when he will get back from Boston. I need a little wagon of some sort to carry my schoolbooks. I'm thinking of a box on wheels with a handle so I can pull it along behind me. Can you help me build it in the evenings?"

"I know just the thing for you. There are some old boxes down at the dock, piled up for whoever wants them. I'll bring one home tomorrow night and all we have to do is add wheels and a handle. Some of them have covers and they look like they will be watertight for rainy days. We can get wheels off the old baby carriage and I can probably get some scrap oak pieces at the shipyard for the tongue and pieces to mount the wheels. I'll bring them home tomorrow night and after supper we can start on it. How does that sound to you?"

To answer his question she walked around the table and planted a kiss on each of his cheeks. Andy stood up and said, "Hey, I'm getting all kinds of kisses here tonight. I'm not used to this stuff."

"Who else has been kissing you, except mother?" Maria asked

"Emily did it first, then you. It doesn't seem like I'm home with the sisters I've always known when they show all this affection so suddenly."

Maria was taken aback and seemed all aghast as she asked, "Emily actually kissed you?"

"Yes, in fact, twice."

"Andy, that's the best news I've heard in a long time. Just think about it, your teasing sister has broken down and come forward with some affection for you. It is sad you will be going away for a long time and everyone will miss you but Emily's showing affection lets us know she really loves her brother when the going is tough. It's really nice."

Melinda walked over to the dining room table where Andy and Maria were having their discussion. She asked Maria to help in the kitchen and asked Andy to find Emily and tell her the dining room table needs to be set for supper. Andy arose from his chair and headed for Emily's room to deliver the message. He found her doing homework from school at a small table.

"Would you help me with this science stuff after supper? I have a hard time getting most of it through my head. Science and math I don't enjoy," she said to Andy.

"Sure, I'll help you but I want to sketch a plan for the book box I promised to make Maria while I still have the idea clear in my mind. I can do it while you're cleaning the table and washing dishes with Maria. After that I'll help you until bedtime, if you want that much help in one evening."

"Oh, Wow!" she exclaimed, adding "I didn't think I'd get so much help all at once."

"Anything for my kid sister," Andy said with a big chuckle to follow.

True to his word Andy helped Emily with her science and math. It seemed simple to him because most boys had a greater interest in those subjects. He at least got Emily locked into a little different way of approaching math and science problems. When the session was over, she thanked him three or four times and he was the recipient of another kiss on his cheek.

Andy went to bed counting down the days he had left to be with the family before the Java Sea headed down river for the open sea. He wanted to go to sea but the change of attitudes with his sisters, especially Emily, gave him some second thoughts about whether it was really what he wanted. He at least knew he had to give it a try to satisfy his longtime yearning to be a sailor. As he thought about it, he realized his doubts would be short lived.

Andy was up early in the morning and walked down to the Java Sea while it was still dark. When he walked into the galley, Mac told him, "You don't have to come this early until the crew gets here later this week."

"I was awoken early by some cattle bawling under my window. I don't know what set them off but they woke me up and I got up and came down here. Furthermore, I didn't want to miss out on anything you and Silas might be doing this early."

"It's too early to miss anything while we're tied to a dock, Andy. At sea it will be different, because most all the jobs are manned around the clock, and in an emergency, they will call all hands to stations to take care of problems. The ship has to be tended around the clock on the open ocean," Mac informed him.

Andy worked with Mac cleaning some kettles, bringing up some fresh water and preparing some vegetables for the day's meals. When he was finished he helped Silas with some painting and tarring of new seizing on the shrouds. They were finished by 2:30 so Andy asked Silas if he could have the rest of the day off to make a box on wheels for his sister's school books. He explained his sister Maria was a teacher at the school and had several books to carry back and forth each day. When Silas told him it was OK for him to go he also explained, Andy was not on the payroll and was free to come and go as he wanted.

Andy walked down the dock and picked up a choice box and cover for his sister's book wagon. He was carrying it on his shoulder when he went into the driveway at the shipyard. He sat it down on the steps to the office and went inside to ask for some oak scraps. A young man he had seen around the waterfront before came over to the front desk and asked if he could help him. Andy explained about the box and what he needed to mount wheels on it.

"Those boxes belong to the shipyard. We make them for farmers to ship apples, potatoes and other such vegetables to the islands. I'll have to sell you the box and oak. We don't have scrap oak. Every little piece can be used for something. I'll give you a good price."

"My sister, Maria Murphy is the teacher at the school and needs a wagon to carry her books to and from home. She has too many to carry in a strap. I told her I would make it for her this week before I go with the Java Sea as cabin boy," Andy explained.

"Did you say your sister's name is Maria Murphy and she teaches at the school?" He asked.

"Yes," Andy replied.

"I know her. She went to school at the same time I did, a couple of classes behind me. My name is Ralph Gleason. Tell her I said hello. She was a nice girl in school. So she became the teacher over there. I'll tell you what I'll do because it is for the school teacher and I knew her as a kid a few years ago. You can have the box and I'll make a replacement when I have some spare time. I can find some hardwood for the handle to pull it along and a couple of pieces of thick fir for the bottom to attach the wheels. How does that sound to you? Of course if you still want oak, I'll have to charge you for it."

"Whatever you can do to help me get a book wagon for my sister I'll appreciate and if you'll trust me, I'll pay you whatever it costs out of my earnings on the Java Sea when we get back from our cruise. How does that sound to you?" Andy proposed to him.

"You know, kid, I like you, and I'll agree to your terms and add something else you might like. We're not busy in the shipyard right now so I'll use my tools to shape the parts you'll need to fit wheels and a drawbar on the box. In fact, I'll put it together for you except for the painting. You or your sister will have to do that. Do we have an agreement?"

"That's real nice of you Mr. Gleason. I'd be silly not to accept your generous offer but I'll need it before the end of the week. I promised my sister."

"If you bring me the wheels in the morning on your way to the Java Sea, I'll more than likely have it done by tomorrow when you go home and you can drag it along with you. That can be part of the agreement."

"How much do you think this will cost when it is done?" Andy asked.

"It won't cost much because I have time to burn until we start a new whaler in the spring. I was planning to build some furniture this winter just to keep busy. My mother needs a new bed frame and there are plenty of other folks here on the peninsula needing furniture, so I expect I will be able to sell whatever I make."

As agreed, the next morning Andy left the carriage wheels on the steps to the shipyard office on his way to the Java Sea. He worked with Silas painting and sealing around the masts where they went through the deck. Silas told him it was a place where leaks often happened because the strain on the masts from the pressure of the sails caused the masts to wiggle a slight amount and the longer a voyage lasted the more water would leak into the ship around the mast. It took all day to dig out the old sealing and replace it with new.

Andy got to the shipyard just as Ralph Gleason was closing up the doors. He told Andy, "I didn't get your book wagon quite finished. I had a couple of interruptions today and had to go to two ships and take measurements for new taff rails. One was damaged in a storm and the other had backed into a dock in Bermuda. Some of these young skippers think they can back into a dock with their square rigged vessels and more than likely, they end up at the shipyard for repairs."

Andy asked, "Do you have it finished enough that I can take it home and finish the work myself?"

"Well, I think so. Most of the work is done. It needs assembly and some screws and bolts tightened. "Do you have any bits, a brace, screwdrivers and wrenches at home," Ralph asked.

"We don't have bits and a brace, but we have several different sizes of gimlets. Will they do?"

"Come with me and we'll go to the tool shed and I'll loan you the bits and brace you need. You can bring them back in the morning.".

"I put all the bolts, nuts and screws in the box. You shouldn't have any trouble assembling it at home. Another pair of hands will help holding parts while you bolt or screw them together."

"My sister Maria said she will help me because the book wagon is for her. It looks to me like we should be able to finish it in a couple of hours because you have everything made and ready to assemble. I sure want to thank you for what you did and I'm sure Maria will be pleased also."

"OK, you're welcome. Just you remember to tell Maria I said, 'Hello, from an old classmate'."

"I promise you I won't forget."

With that, Andy loaded the box with all the wagon parts inside on his shoulder and started walking home.

When he went in the house everyone was nearly finished eating their supper and his mother got up and dished up a fresh, hot plate for Andy while he washed his hands. She asked him, "How's our sailor boy tonight?"

"I'm fine, Mom," he replied. "I have a message for Maria from one of her old classmates. He is running the shipyard where I got the parts for the book wagon. It is already to put together and Maria and I can do it after we eat. Today I helped Silas caulk around the masts and peeled some onions and potatoes for Mac. It was a busy day and the caulking work was kind of dirty when your hands got stuck up with the tar. We washed it off with turpentine. I had a couple of scratches from yesterday's sail sewing that really smarted and burned when the turpentine hit them. Mac gave me some stuff he called soft soap and once I washed with that the sting from the turpentine went away."

"What I want to know is who sent me a message, and what does it say?" Maria said.

"Oh, it's from the guy at the shipyard. He went to school at the same time you did but was a couple of grades ahead of you. His name is Gleason. I think he said his first name was Ralph. He wanted me to tell you 'Hello, from an old classmate'."

"I think I remember him. I believe he quit school after the eighth grade. He was a quiet boy and seemed to be out of place as the only member of the eighth grade. I guess he couldn't think of going to school for four more years as the only student in the class. Quitting after the eighth grade often happens in one room schoolhouses," Maria told Andy, while everyone was still sitting at the table and privy to the conversation.

When Daniel Murphy offered to help his wife Melinda clean up and do the dishes so the three Murphy children could go to work on the book wagon, they all jumped at the chance to get out of the kitchen chore and work in the barn. Andy lit two lanterns and with each of the girls carrying one, the three went out the door. By following Ralph's instructions, help from the girls holding things in place while he bored holes and screwed parts together, they were finished in a little over an hour and a half. Maria was real pleased with the book wagon and said she was going to stop and see Ralph some day to thank him personally.

"I could use one of these for my books," Emily said.

"You won't need one," Maria told her, "You can put your books in here and we can haul it home together. The handle is made for two people."

"That's a good idea. I don't want to go begging to Ralph again," Andy told them.

CHAPTER 7

▼

Two days after Andy and his sisters finished building and painting the book wagon, Andy went to the Java Sea for the day. Mac advised him he should bring some things from his sea bag and start living aboard as of the next day. "We have a few of the crew coming on today and tomorrow. There will be more work for you which must be finished each day, meaning you won't have time to go home at night. I'll make sure you get at least one more day to see your family before we sail."

"OK." Andy replied, then asked, "When do you think we will sail?"

"Captain Murphy told me he expects we will sail Thursday or Friday afternoon on the outgoing tide. The tides are higher than normal this week and are called flood tides. When they ebb they go out with a stronger flow. If we go out on one of them we can reach the open sea in less time. Understand?"

"I have heard of flood tides before. I also learned about them in a book I read about sailing. I just didn't know a ship could go faster by sailing on one. It does make sense to me, going in the direction the water is moving would be faster for the ship, too."

"You got it."

Andy started for home just as the girls were going home from school. He walked the last half mile to the farm watching them, each pulling on one side of the book wagon's tongue. He asked how the book wagon was working out as a carrier of school books and papers. Walking beside Maria, she threw her arm across his shoulders and told him it was a perfect wagon for the job. She and Emily both talked about how much easier it was to get their books home and thanked him over and over for building it for them.

Maria said, "We stopped at the shipyard last night on the way home from school and thanked Ralph Gleason for his part in the building of the book wagon. He was real pleased it came out so well. He said you did a good job of putting it together and that Emily and I did a good job on the painting. He joked about me becoming a painter in his shipyard. He's grown up a lot since I last saw him in the eighth grade at school. I like the way he is now."

"That isn't the end of the story either," added Emily. She told Andy, "He asked Maria to go out to supper with him next Saturday evening. He wants to take her to a special restaurant in Annapolis."

Turning to Maria she asked, "What did he say the name of the place was in Annapolis?"

Maria answered, "The Green Lion Inn."

"Wait a minute," said Andy. "That's a tough seafront tavern and I don't think you should go there."

"Ralph told us there is a Green Lyon Tavern, not fit for ladies and gentlemen to go to, but The Green Lion Inn is a classy, new restaurant with French Cuisine. It opened last spring," Maria said.

"Well, I never heard of that place. Ralph seems to be a good man and I guess he wouldn't take you to an unfit restaurant. I was just kind of worried about my sister." Andy responded.

"I feel sure it is okay and I will talk it over with mother and father before I tell him I will go with him. If they don't approve, I'll tell him I can't go and it would be better if we just have a picnic on Sunday afternoon, somewhere nice, along the river."

"She'll go." Emily told Andy. "You should have seen the two of them when they met. They were like the lost lovers you hear about. He couldn't take his eyes off her and was all gushy about seeing her again. I wouldn't be surprised, if she goes with him, the next thing you hear is wedding bells."

"Or maybe I can get him interested in going back to school and completing his education. Did you ever think of that as a motive?" Maria challenged her sister. "I may even tutor him."

The girls went in the house to help Melinda Murphy preparing supper. Andy took the book wagon to the barn and talked to his father, who was just finishing the milking chores. He scooped a measure of grain from the grain bins, took it to the cow for a treat after she had been milked. He told his father he had important news about the sailing and wanted to talk to the family after super.

"I will make sure they listen to whatever you have to say," said his father Daniel Murphy.

"Thank you, Dad. I have to move aboard ship tomorrow. As soon as we finish loading in two or three days, we are heading down river in the afternoon, taking advantage of the outgoing tide. I have been busy the last couple of days and may get home one more night before we leave. Mac, the cook said he would try to get me home one more night, but made no promises because most all the crew will be aboard tomorrow. He said, 'All but the usual two or three stragglers should be here'."

"We'll miss you around here, son. It is important for you to learn something you can use to earn a living when times are hard. There always seems to be a demand for seafaring men when others are going hungry. Be real careful and pay attention to what the best of the crewmen teach you. Remember, you are always welcome to come home and work on the farm with me. That said, let's go in and eat."

Andy stepped over in front of his father, threw his arms around him as far as they would reach and with very misty eyes said, "I love my home and family Dad, it's just a yearning inside of me to go to sea, I want to fulfill it. If it doesn't work, I might take you up on your offer to come home to the farm."

As the two walked in the back door Melinda Murphy excitedly exclaimed, "Andy's home for supper, put another plate on the table." Then she turned to Andy and said, "Son, it's good to see you tonight. I've been praying all day you'd come home tonight. I was talking to Priscilla Driscoll this morning. She told me Tom told her the Java Sea was loading cargo and only had a couple of day's loading sitting on the dock. Is that right?"

"I think so, Mom. They have stevedores and some of the crew working on it. I don't know how long it will take them to load it all, but they loaded a lot of it today, and tomorrow is the day the rest of the crew come aboard. I think we will sail in about three days."

As the family moved to take their seats around the table, Maria took the seat beside her mother where her brother usually sat. When Melinda asked her why she had taken Andy's usual place, Maria replied, "To force Andy across the table from you so you can have a better chance to watch him on his last night at home."

With that, Daniel Murphy instructed the family to hold hands around the table as he said the blessing before the meal. Once their hands were joined Daniel said a prayer very much different than the family was used to hearing at mealtime. It was deep and thoughtful with simple thanks to a loving God. When asked by Melinda why he had said that particular prayer he explained he thought his best prayer should be said on a night when his son was leaving for sea with an unknown world ahead of him.

"I liked it," said Emily. "Where did you learn it, Father?

"When I was a boy, there was an Indian family lived across the creek from my family's cabin. The oldest member of their family was the great grandfather. He taught it to me and his great grandson while we played together as children. He said it was his 'Great Prayer.' Once I had learned it, I never forgot it. If any of you would like to learn it, I'll write it down so you can study the words."

Melinda and Maria went to the kitchen and came back with a warm apple pie for dessert. Emily cleaned the table of the dinner plates. She noticed everyone had finished their food, with no leftovers or scraps to discard. The family all liked Melinda's good home cooking, and meals usually ended with clean plates.

"Wow, Mom, Apple pie, that's my favorite!" exclaimed Andy.

After the family had finished eating the pie, there came a knock on the back kitchen door. "Andy, will you see who that is knocking," asked Melinda?

When Andy opened the door, he was surprised to see Jimmy Mixon standing on the stoop with his sea bag leaning against the railing. "Come on in," he told Jimmy. "We're just finishing our supper."

Melinda spoke first. "Well, Hello stranger. Come in, sit yourself down and have a piece of fresh made apple pie. What brings you this way at this time of day?"

"I am heading out to the old house we lived in before my folks moved to the Boston area. I have to pick up a box of my belongings they left there for me. The folks renting the farm agreed to take care of my things until I could come for them."

"By the time you get out there it will be too late to knock on their door tonight," Daniel Murphy told him. "Why don't you stay here with us tonight and go out in the morning?" He asked.

"I wouldn't want to put you folks out. You have been very helpful and good to me already. I could wear out my welcome. I wouldn't want that either. I enjoy coming to visit here."

Daniel Murphy told him, "Andy wants to talk to the family now that we are finished eating. I'll gather everyone here at the dining room table and we will hear what he has to say, then work out something to help you get on your way to solving your problem."

Once the family was gathered around the table again, Daniel told everyone Andy wants to talk to all of them as a family group. "He says he has something to tell us and I want everyone to listen because he will be leaving soon and we'll have to get used to him not being here every day."

As Andy started to talk, his voice choked up on him and his eyes watered. He managed to hold his composure long enough to let everyone know he loved them and would be leaving early in the morning with his sea bag. He was not sure he would get home again before the Java Sea sailed.

Jimmy Mixon told everyone this was the moment when it was the most difficult for the family and the sailor. "Emotions run high," he said. "My family went through this at least six times in the past ten years. It's never easy. It gets easier with time. The first time is always the hardest. Andy, you are going on a good ship with a top-notch captain. I'll look forward to your return and hearing about your many days at sea, the ports you visited, your adventures, most people are never aware of in their lifetime. Good Luck, kid."

Emily started crying. Maria had tears running down her cheeks and Melinda Murphy was trying to calm the girls emotions while holding back all her own.

Andy got up, walked around the table and after planting a kiss on each sister's cheek, stood between his parents and with an arm around each one and said, "Mom and Dad, I love you and I'm proud of being your son. I'll do the best I can to bring credit to the family name."

Daniel Murphy started sniffling a little as Melinda headed for the bedroom, with tears really flowing now between the soft wails she was no longer able to hold back. All she could think of was her little boy going to sea. She knew a sailor's life was a hard life and now, she suddenly learned what a hard life it was for those left behind on the shore.

With the family exiting to spend their time alone to regain their composure, Andy and Jimmy Mixon found themselves together looking across the dining room table wearing confused looks. Andy spoke first, "I'm not sure I should go, now that everyone is taking it so hard," he told Jimmy.

"This is just the way it is in close families. You've got to go if you ever expect to be your own man. They'll get over it in a few days, and you will too. If you really want to be a sailor like your Uncle Fred, you have to stand strong when confronted with conditions you are not necessarily in agreement with," Jimmy said.

"I know you're right. It's just my fondness for my family. I don't like to see them all upset over something I am doing. I'll do it, with a lot of misgivings."

"Now you're talking," Jimmy said.

Several minutes later the door to the parents' room opened and both Melinda and Daniel came back into the dining room. Andy and Jimmy had taken it upon themselves to clean up after the meal and were finishing the job in the kitchen as Melinda approached with a surprised look. "What are you boys doing, cleaning up after supper," she asked?

Jimmy answered her question in a falsetto voice when he replied, "I'm a cabin boy and Andy is going to be one. This was a perfect time for me to teach him some of the tricks of the trade. He'll do fine with a few days practice on the Java Sea. The hardest thing he will have to learn is how to walk a moving deck with a loaded tray in his hands."

"Jimmy gave me some good tips about being a cabin boy. I think I can handle the job with his teaching and Mac's coaching."

"Dad and I want to apologize for breaking down the way we did. It's almost like we didn't support our son's decisions to become a seafaring man on his Uncle Fred's ship," explained Melinda.

"I understand, Mom. Jimmy and I have been talking while you were in the bedroom and he explained to me about the pressure you and Dad feel about a young son going to sea. I put myself in your place and realize what you're thinking. Jimmy said it's because you love me and I like that idea."

Arrangements were discussed and agreed that Jimmy could rent Andy's room while he was gone. He could do the farm work Andy normally did to pay for his meals. Jimmy liked the idea. He told them, "If I am successful in buying property down river, I'll be spending a lot of my time preparing it for a homestead by building a home and farm buildings." He agreed he would keep up the work Andy was leaving behind.

CHAPTER 8

▼

At four the next morning Andy quietly went out the back door with his sea bag balanced on his shoulder. He tried not to wake anyone but the door slipped from his grip, slamming against the casing. Almost immediately his mother was there beside him, telling him she wanted to walk part way to the ship, so she could spend a little more time with him. He tried to discourage her from going out in the dark so early in the morning, but she insisted she would be alright, and would not go far from home before coming back.

She walked beside him with one hand on his shoulder, rubbing gently as she talked. "Andy, I was really worried last night about you leaving. Your father and I had a good talk before we went to sleep and he assured me that his brother was a very good sailor and ship's master. Fred has been a ship Captain for over twelve years now and has always had successful voyages. I trust the voyage you are going on will be a success too."

They walked a few yards and Andy stopped, taking his sea bag off his shoulder and setting it on the ground in a grassy spot beside the roadbed. He looked at his mother and in a stern voice said, "Mom, you have to go back home. I don't want you out wandering around this early in the morning all alone. I got enough to worry about without worrying if you get home safely."

Melinda agreed to return home as he wished. She threw her arms around him, giving him a big strong hug, saying, "OK, son, all I want is for you to promise me you'll be real careful while you're gone."

As she turned to walk back home, he said, "I will, Mom."

Andy shouldered his sea bag again and walked toward the Java Sea, thinking about the loving mother he was leaving as he went to fulfill his own destiny. He thought about his Dad, Maria and Emily and realized he had a good family he was leaving behind. He also thought about Jimmy Mixon and wondered how he would get along with the two Murphy sisters. He chuckled to himself as it crossed his mind that Maria had a dinner date with Ralph Gleason and with Jimmy Mixon back in the picture he wondered if a lovers' triangle would develop.

For the next two days the stevedores and crew worked hard, long hours loading cargo, allowing for each consignment to be unloaded at different ports of call, making room to load cargo they were to pick up. Andy asked Silas why the cotton bales were loaded on top of the other cargo with big spaces between them. Silas explained that certain types of cargo had to be loaded with plenty of expansion room in case it got wet. "If those bales were packed tight and got wet in stormy weather they could swell enough to damage the ship. Stored deep in the hold, it would be difficult to work them out and the swelling could burst the planking on the sides of the ship," he told him.

"Wow," Andy said, using one of his favorite expressions. "Now I can understand why special handling is necessary for cotton."

Andy learned more in time. Cargo ship crews have to be very careful how they load their cargo. Loads have to be tied down so they don't move around when the ship is sailing in heavy weather, some cargos have to be cribbed, meaning a framework of strong lumber has to be built around the cargo to hold it firmly in place. Protecting the ship, which protects the crew, is the first consideration when loading cargo. If they were loading highly combustible or non compatible cargo the crew would use different holds to keep things separated.

Andy would learn much more about a sea-going cargo vessel's loading and off loading, he had never given thought to before. At mealtime he would learn by listening to the crew as he carried bowls of food from the galley to the tables. Some cargos had to be kept dry and it was a difficult job to maintain watertight integrity on a wooden sailing ship. He learned that some ships hauling lime caught fire when the lime got wet. Others were saved by covering the hatches with canvas and making the hold air tight smothering the flames. Some lime ships burned to the waterline. Others burned and sank. The cargo alone could be a perilous thing if it wasn't stored and handled properly. As he learned about cargo handling, he gained more respect for the officers who planned and directed the loading.

On his second night on board he became acquainted with a couple of the new arrivals. One was a man named Willie Wispor who said he was a Canadian and came to the Java Sea to watch her crew work. He had heard rumors of how good a crew the Java Sea had and he didn't believe anyone was "that good" at handling a ship, especially a cargo ship with three masts on the South American run. He believed Canadian crews were the best and he was going to prove no American crew was superior. After his first cruise on the Java Sea, he decided it really did have the best crew. He just kept signing over on her.

Willie Wispor was a man of medium build and probably about twenty-eight to thirty years of age. He had big sideburns on an otherwise clean shaven face. His hair was somewhat curly but a little too long in Andy's opinion. Noticing his hands, Andy wondered why they were not as rough and calloused as the other members of the climbing crew who were the ones responsible for handling the royals, tops and sky-sails at the tops of the masts. When Andy mentioned to Mac what he had noticed about Willie's hands, Mac said, "When the men go aloft to tend sail, you watch Willie, see how many lines he handles compared to the others. I think the only reason he is a part of the Java Sea's crew is because he is a good man at sewing sail, splicing rope, standing wheel watches and keeping a close watch on the horizons for other ships. He has a knack for spotting sails long before anyone else sees them."

"How can he see sails out near the horizon before anyone else?" Andy asked as he pondered what Mac had said.

"I don't know how he does it, but he must have some hidden ability to see a different shade of gray between the horizon mist and the color of gray sail. I only know he has spotted a sail way out on the horizon long before anyone else can see it. All he says is he doesn't understand why the rest of the crew can't see a sail just like he does. He's a strange one, that Willie," Mac said.

About mid-afternoon, while cleaning in the Captain's cabin, Andy heard Mac and Silas arguing on the deck above him. He would catch pieces of the argument but not enough to put together and make sense of what they were saying. Right after the evening meal he learned what it was all about.

Silas came down in the galley where Andy and Mac were finishing the cleanup. He told them he wanted to talk to them, "Right now," he said.

"What's got your feathers all ruffled, you old crow," Mac taunted him.

"I want to get it straightened out about the boy going home tonight for the last time. We're leaving on the morning tide and a couple of hours at home will be a sad couple of hours for him and his whole family. I don't think he should go home. If it was up to me, I'd tell him what it's all about and keep him aboard the ship." Silas said in a heated sort of way.

"Why don't we let the lad decide what's best? Mac responded. Then turning to Andy he said, "I told you I'd try to get you home for a little more time with your family. Silas disagrees with me on the matter. What do you think?"

"Whatever is best for the ship and the rest of the crew is what I think is best," Andy replied.

"Spoken like a true sailor," Silas shouted, somewhat gleefully.

"As I see the problem, son, if you go home and tell everyone you're leaving on the morning tide you will have them all upset, crying and everything else. You left home three mornings ago and they are getting used to you being gone. Going back now is just adding fuel to the fire and making it tougher on them and you. I think, in the best interests of you and your family, it will be better if you just sail on down the river and write them a letter which you can mail in Charleston. That's my advice," Silas advised Andy.

Andy turned to Mac and said, "I think Silas is right. I don't want to go home and watch my mother and sisters cry because I have a job on a ship. I guess it will be best if I stay aboard like the rest of the crew."

With everyone satisfied with the outcome, they each went back to his own specific chores, getting the ship ready to cast off from the dock in the morning. Silas went back to the sail locker and helped Willie Wispor finish some patching while Mac worked in the galley cleaning up a few more things and preparing for an early breakfast. Andy took a pot of coffee and went to the Captain's cabin to refill the Captains coffee-keeper urn. He let himself in as quietly as he could. Captain Murphy was sitting at his desk going over some charts when Andy walked in. He spoke first, asking Andy, "Are you ready to go to sea in the morning?"

"Yes, sir, Captain Murphy," he replied with his best cabin boy attitude.

"Mac and Silas have both been telling me they think you will work out fine in the position you're in and with a little time at sea you will show improvement for promotion. I was pleased to hear that. I want you to know as soon as promotions are available, and you are qualified, there is nothing to prevent you from moving up on the Java Sea. It's all up to you, plus experience and time. Good Luck, Andy, Good sailing," Captain Murphy told his new cabin boy and nephew.

The next morning Mac shook Andy awake and whispered in his ear it was time to get breakfast started. The two of them dressed and left the crew's quarters for the galley where they would work hard for the next couple of hours cooking a big breakfast for the crew when they got up at 5:30. Andy started by making a big pot of coffee, then came the setting of tables with plates, utensils, cups and condiments like sugar, salt and pepper. Another thing which Andy thought was odd for the breakfast meal was a jar of mustard. Some of the sailors put mustard on their hash-brown potatoes in the morning so Mac made sure Andy put a jar on the table.

Once the crew tables were set for breakfast, Andy took his first pot of coffee to the Captain's Cabin and prepared to awaken Captain Murphy. As soon as he stepped in the door, the Captain greeted him with a cheery, "Good Morning, Andy."

"Good morning. Captain Murphy, sir."

"The tide will be turning in about an hour and we'll be letting go the dock for our trip down river on the outgoing tide. There will be a lot of action on deck when we're getting under way. You should stay clear of the main deck until everything has settled down. I wouldn't want you to get injured before we get out of the harbor because you got in the way of some wildly flying rope," Captain Murphy advised him.

"Thank you, Captain Murphy, sir, I'll be careful. I'll bring your breakfast right away. Is there anything else you want right now," Andy asked?

"You can tell Mac I only want a small, light breakfast this morning. He'll know what I mean. That'll be all, Andy," the Captain told him as he moved toward the door to leave.

When Andy told Mac the Captain wanted a small, light breakfast, Mac said, "Yep, we're going to sea, alright. He always orders a small, light breakfast when we're sailing. It's his way of dieting to take off the pounds he puts on when we're tied to a dock and he's not working hard enough to keep extra weight off. He must have gained a few pounds while we were in port."

"I'll have something ready for him in about 15 minutes and you can take it to him," Mac added.

"I'll work on the cleanup in the crew's mess while I'm waiting. When it is ready you can find me there," Andy told him as he headed for the crew's mess to start the cleanup. As soon as he walked in the door he noticed Captain Murphy sitting with four other men in the far corner of the mess compartment.

The Captain said, "Andy, I'll take my breakfast right here. I have to talk to these men to explain what we need done when we let go the dock. There are several new members in the crew and these men will have to watch over them, as well as do their own jobs, when we head down the river. Safety will be our first requirement. We don't need anyone getting hurt because he isn't familiar with the Java Sea and her style of rigging. Some of the lines get running pretty fast as they make their way through the blocks. We don't want someone on the deck pinned between the mast or the rail and a fast moving, taught line. He could be injured badly, possibly needing hospitalization for the injuries."

Andy moved to the other side of the crew's mess and had not cleaned a single table when Mac called him to say the Captain's breakfast was ready. Andy went in the galley and picked up the tray with a steaming cup of freshly made coffee. As he was carrying it to the Captain's table, one of the new crewmen reached out and took the cup of coffee off the tray in one clean, swooping motion. Andy stopped in his tracks and told the man, "That's the Captain's coffee."

"It's mine, now," he replied.

Andy straightened himself up to his full height, looked the man fully in the eye and with his deepest and gruffest sounding voice told him, "You heard me. I said it is the Captain's coffee. Now put it back."

The man merely laughed at Andy and made no move to return the coffee to the tray. Almost immediately Mac appeared in the galley doorway, holding an oversized meat cleaver and said, "You heard the boy, Rosco. Put the coffee back on the tray."

Rosco Quinn suddenly stopped laughing and returned the coffee to Andy's tray, with a half apology to Mac by saying, "Aw, Mac, I was only joshing the boy."

"I don't think you were joshing until I showed up with my trusty cleaver," Mac told him.

Andy finished cleaning up the crews mess and was helping Mac with the galley cleaning when he heard a screeching sound coming from the after deck. He asked Mac what it was and he told him it was the after mooring line squeaking against the dock bollards as the ship got underway. "You mean we're moving," Andy asked?

"That's right Andy, we will soon be underway, once they let go the last line to the dock," Mac informed him.

"Can I go take a look," Andy asked?

"Sure," Mac replied. Just come back about 1030 to help with the noon meal."

Andy didn't have to be told twice, he went bounding up the closest ladder onto the deck to watch the Java Sea head down river toward the open sea for his first voyage. He was excited and tried to see everything that was happening all at once. The first thing he heard was the bos'n' mate's call to let go all lines forward. Within seconds the Java Sea's bow started to swing away from the dock and turn toward the middle of the river.

Next came the cry to ease off aft, "Slowly, men, Slowly," called the Bos'n' as the ship was pivoted around on the stern mooring line to where she was pointed straight across the river. "More slack on the stern line," was ordered.

"Set the skysails and royals on the fore and mizzen masts," was called out by someone on the poop deck.

Andy noticed the Java Sea had made a complete turnaround in the river before letting go her last mooring line to the dock. She was now heading down river along with the tide. He looked back toward the dock the Java Sea had just left. His mother, father and both of his sisters were standing where the ship had been tied up, waving a farewell to the new cabin boy. He waved back with a lump in his throat, because he had never before waved goodbye to them.

Soon the Java Sea was sailing smoothly with the current in the river helping her along and with the uppermost sails set, they began to billow a little which meant she was getting a little assistance from the wind. Andy watched as the shoreline changed and the ship picked up speed, slowly at first, then with a real noticeable motion when compared to the shore.

Andy's mind was racing with excitement and thoughts kept coming faster than he could put them in perspective. I'm a cabin boy...Uncle Fred's ship...Java Sea...Jimmy Mixon...sky sails...Mom & Dad...let go aft...Maria, Emily...Silas...Mac...more slack on the stern line...put the coffee back...neighbors, the Driscolls...Ralph Gleason, date with Maria...Willie Wispor...royals...gallants...Mac called and told Andy it was time to work on the noon meal.

Although Andy was enjoying himself watching the Java Sea moving down river at a faster and faster speed, he knew when Mac called he was responsible for helping with galley work as a first order of his duties. He reluctantly left his sightseeing and went to work in the galley. Mac had a good noon meal started with two roasts of beef in the oven. Because of it, the galley was hot, and coming in from the deck where he had been watching two crewmen steer the ship, with the big double wheel that moved the rudder, he started to break out in a sweat. As soon as his forehead began to run sweat, Mac provided him with an improvised sweatband made from an old apron, telling him he better get used to going from outside into the hot galley because it was something he would be doing on a daily basis. "You need to carry a sweatband in your pocket for just such times," he said.

When all was ready for the crew to eat, Mac told Andy to go tell Silas he could send the first shift down to eat. Andy didn't hesitate. He ran up the ladder from the mess deck to the main deck and got a good view as he wandered around looking for Silas. There were more sails set, the speed was faster, with the bend of the river only a few yards ahead. The excitement of his first voyage was building in Andy.

He found Silas on the fo'c'sle teaching a couple of new seamen how to coil down a line so it would run out without becoming tangled. When he told him the noon meal was ready for the first shift, Silas thanked him and said he would round up the first ten men and send them right down. When Andy said there was room for fifteen to eat on the first shift, Silas said, "I don't want too many away from their stations at one time until we get away from the shore and clear the river into the open sea."

Andy started back for the galley, paying particular attention to how the ship was beginning to move up and down over a small ground swell rolling into the mouth of the river. He noticed her sails and how many were already set. When he got back to the galley, Mac told him the Captain's meal would be ready in just a minute and for him to wait to deliver it before he got busy with any of the other work. He watched as Mac put the final touches on the tray and poured a cup of coffee, setting it in the middle of the tray where it would be safer from spillage when Andy went to the Captain's cabin with it.

When Mack gave him the OK, he picked up the tray and headed aft. As he walked in the Captain's cabin his uncle Fred was sitting on a stool, making notes on some charts spread before him on a large table. Andy asked where he wanted him to set his food and Captain Murphy replied, "Let me swing these charts around sideways and you can put it on the end of this table."

As soon as Andy placed the tray down, Captain Murphy immediately took the cup of coffee and put it to his lips for a taste, saying, "One thing about old Mac, he sure as heck knows how to brew a good cup of coffee." After a short pause for another swallow of the coffee, Captain Murphy said, "As soon as Mac releases you from your noontime work, I'd like you to come down here and I'll teach you about the charts and the ports we will be visiting on this voyage. I think you'll find it interesting."

Andy replied, "Yes Sir, Captain Murphy, it sounds like it will be interesting, I'll probably be back in a couple of hours. Is there anything else I can do for you while I am here?"

As Andy came back to the upper deck, he noticed there was more movement of the ship and the deck had a small tilt to it, which he later learned was a normal listing to port or starboard when they were at sea with the sails set and working. The Java Sea had cleared the river mouth, the land was falling away astern, the sails continued to gather more wind, there was more creaking in the rigging as she headed into open seas, gaining speed. Andy had a bout with melancholy which disappeared quickly when he got back to the galley and Mac started giving him orders about what to work on next.

CHAPTER 9

---▼---

On his second day at sea, Andy awoke with a few shakes from Mac. His thoughts turned to his first day and how much he had learned, how excited he felt about this new adventure as cabin boy on the Java Sea. The biggest difference he noticed was the ship was moving up and down more between rolls from side to side. His stomach felt a little strange, like he was becoming sick. He got dressed, even though it was somewhat of a struggle, and headed to the galley.

As soon as he walked in the door, Mac passed him a cup of something to drink. "What's this?" he asked, staring into the cup of greenish looking liquid.

"That's an herb concoction for new sailors until they get used to the roll and pitch of the ship. We don't need a seasick cabin boy as long as we have the means to keep his tummy calm," Mac told him.

"I'm not seasick," he protested.

"You may think you're not, but you are almost as green as the seaweed in that cup. Now, drink up and you'll feel better within the hour."

Still protesting, Andy drank it. Mac made sure he drained the cup, and sure enough, Mac was right, Andy did feel better within an hour.

Andy approached Mac after breakfast, with the cleanup finished and said, "You were right about me feeling better if I drank that green stuff. I feel good now. What was in the cup," he asked?

"Trust me kid, you don't want to know," Mac said. "At least not now," he added.

"I have the right to know what I drank, don't I?" Andy said.

"Someday I'll tell you," was all he could get Mac to say.

"Is there anything else you want me to do before I leave," Andy asked?

"I believe I can handle everything until it is time to start the noon meal. You can help Silas with his bo's'n mate's work and learn a little from him, if that's possible," Mac informed him.

Andy chuckled to himself at Mack's ending remark and the tone of voice he said it with. He realized then and there, there's a lot of jealousy between these two men with the obvious friction they play back and forth between themselves. He also made up his mind it was mostly in jest so one could tease the other. As he turned to leave, Mac reminded him to take another cup of coffee to the Captain and see if he needed anything.

"Aye, aye, Sir," Andy said in a jesting manner.

"Now don't you start being funny with me like your good buddy Silas, or I'll keep you in the galley twenty-four hours a day, with a scrubber in each hand."

"I was just joking with you," Andy said, taken aback by Mac's threat.

"I know that. And, I was just joking with you about scrubbers in both hands. But, while we're at it, you should know, some guys can't be joked with, and some get angry as all get out if you try to tease or joke with them. So, I guess my best advice to you is, go slow with the joking until you become friends with the other man. Then, if it will be a jesting relationship, like Silas and I, it will come naturally. Good Luck!"

Andy picked up a tray, placed a large cup of steaming coffee on it and headed for Captain Murphy's cabin. When he walked in the door with the tray and coffee, the Captain greeted him with a cheerful, "Hello, Andy, you're a man after my own heart, bringing me a big cup of coffee right at this time."

"Thank you, Captain Murphy, Sir," Andy said. "Will there be anything else you need?"

"Come over here a minute and I'll give you a briefing on what these charts mean and why we have so many of them on the ship." Captain Murphy told him.

Andy went over to the chart table and stood beside his uncle as he unrolled a large chart and placed it on the table with some books to hold the corners down. "This," he said, "is a chart of the Atlantic Ocean north of the equator. The lines running up and down are longitudes and the cross lines are latitudes. They are laid out in degrees and the ship's navigator can determine our location by using a sextant to figure out our position on the earth. His job requires a lot of mathematical figuring and information from several sets of navigator's scales and tables. Our first stop will be here in Charleston, South Carolina. From there we'll go to Port of Spain, Trinidad, located right here, then head south along the South American coast which is shown on a different chart."

The Captain pulled out a different and smaller chart, placing it on top of the large one he had been showing Andy. "Now this is a coastal chart," he said. "It is used when you are going into a harbor or port. This is the one for Charleston and we will be going through this opening into the harbor and tying up to one of the docks. Their harbor master will tell us which one, once we get inside the harbor itself. These small numbers scattered around the harbor and its approaches are depth markings to tell us how much water depth we can expect at any given point as we sail to the dock. These charts are marked with water depth at either high tide or low tide and there is a notation to add or subtract a certain number of feet depending on the rise and fall of the tide."

"Well, Andy what do you think of the information I told you about navigating," Captain Murphy asked?

"It sounds complicated. I'd like to learn to do it if I may, "Andy replied.

"I'll talk to Lieutenant Brown, our navigator and see if he would like to give you some lessons two or three days a week when time allows."

"Gosh, that's great, Captain Murphy, Sir," Andy told him.

"I really don't need anything else this morning, so you can go do your regular job now, Andy."

"Thank you, Captain. If you need me I'll be working with Silas until we prepare the noon meal."

"That's fine, Andy. Be sure and pay good attention to whatever Silas teaches you. He's a good man and knows much more than most sailors do about their ships and sailing. He could be a Master if he would make application for his Captain's papers. There are new ship designs being talked about and if they build them, they will probably be the kind of ship where Silas would like to be in command. The new ships will be called "Clipper Ships." I expect it will be several more years before they are commonly seen. Some people are calling them racing ships because they will be much faster than the Java Sea type ships."

For the next two days Andy learned to splice ropes while he was working with Silas and had a chance to make biscuits while working in his galley job. Although his biscuits were a little overcooked, the crew ate them without complaint, probably thinking Mac had been the creator and they didn't dare to complain about his cooking or they might get worse.

Just before noon the following day, Andy noticed a number of sea birds were present and looking ahead on the horizon he could see a dark streak of what a short while later turned out to be land. When he asked Willie Wispor the helmsman, about it, he was told, "We're going into Charleston Harbor this afternoon. We'll drop anchor in the harbor and tie up to the dock in the morning."

As the Java Sea headed in toward the harbor a smaller, outbound coastal sail ship came within hailing distance of the port side and her captain called out to the Java Sea, warning of a shift in the barrier reef at the entrance of the harbor.

"Ahoy, on the three mast ship," they called. When answered by Captain Murphy, they informed him, "You better stay about a quarter of a league south of the Channel Marker because the sand barrier has been moved by the storms we've been having in this area. None of the charts are right and they haven't moved the buoys."

"Thank you for the advice. It was nice of you to come within hailing distance to let us know about the problem," Captain Murphy called back.

"You're welcome, but I didn't want you running aground, swinging around and blocking what channel we have left. Good Luck and fair weather to you."

"The same to you," Captain Murphy called back as the smaller, schooner rigged ship veered off to port and headed in a southeasterly direction.

Captain Murphy said, "Get Lieutenant Brown up here and tell him to bring the chart of Charleston Harbor from my desk."

Not knowing exactly who the Captain was talking to, because he hadn't directed the order to anyone specifically, Andy decided to go and get the Lieutenant. When he returned to the wheel deck, Captain Murphy told him it was good to see he was willing to take the initiative when a general order was given.

"I didn't know who was supposed to go and as nobody else seemed to be going, I just thought it was probably up to me to go."

"Well, Andy, you did the right thing. That's what you should have done. You're the cabin boy and errands are all part of your job," the Captain told him.

Lieutenant Brown showed up with the chart of Charleston Harbor and Captain Murphy turned to him and they discussed where best to make the approach based on the warning received from the other craft. They decided it would be a good idea to put a man on the heaving lead to take depth soundings as they neared the area where the sandbar should shoal up. Silas was informed and the leadsman's platform was rigged over the starboard bow in readiness for taking soundings as they got closer to the sand bar.

Andy went up on the wheel deck and Willie Wispor was still on watch keeping the ship on course with the big steering wheel which controlled the rudder. He liked watching Willie when he was on duty coning the ship. His head had just popped above the deck line when Willie said, "Hi, Andy. What are you up to today?"

"Oh, I'm just nosing around, seeing what I can learn. I have to help Mac pretty soon in the galley."

"If you want to learn something, go up forward and watch them heave the lead to measure the depth of the water as we sail in through the bar. This is the first time it has been necessary on this trip and from what the other ship told us, it looks like we have to find a new entrance to the harbor," Willie told him.

"Thanks, Willie. I'm on my way," Andy told him as he turned back toward the main deck.

Andy arrived on the forward deck just in time to see Rosco Quinn walk out on the leadsman's platform and heave the first of his soundings. Rosco was using a heavy lead sinker with a cup like end on the bottom and a hole for the heaving line at the top. He held his arm over the side of the platform railing and swung the weight back and forth until it was swinging quite a large arc above the water. When he had swung it about four times he let it go on the forward swing in such a way it landed ahead of the bow and sank quickly to the bottom. On the first swing, all the line ran out and the lead didn't hit bottom. Rosco called out, "No bottom."

Several tries later he called, "By the mark, Five fathoms." It was followed by three soundings of four fathoms and then back to the five fathoms mark for several readings. Suddenly there was a slowing of the ship speed and a loud crunching sound as the Java Sea momentarily straightened up then started a slight list toward the port side.

Captain Murphy, who had come to the wheel deck called out, "Bring her over hard to port, Willie. The channel must have moved farther south than the schooner folks said.

Slowly the Java Sea righted herself and then gradually leaned on the starboard tack as she had been before the grounding. Silas filled the cup on the bottom of the heaving lead with tallow and told Rosco to take some soundings to see what kind of bottom we had scraped. When the lead came up with sand and small pieces of seashell, it was decided there was not much chance of severe damage to the under side of the Java Sea.

Later, after all was well and the ship was on her course into the harbor, Andy went down to the Galley to help Mac start on the evening meal. As he went through the dining area he saw Captain Murphy and Lt. Brown discussing the Charleston harbor chart. Lt. Brown called him over to where they were seated. "Andy'" he said, "Take a look at this chart. It shows the channel markers and channel into Charleston Harbor. If you learn navigation, you must remember a chart can be wrong, not because of the chart maker, but because the sea bottom is always changing. It happens mostly at the mouth of a river or in areas where strong ocean currents move the bottom around, especially the lighter sediments like sand and mud. We were more than a mile south of the channel marker when we grounded. It was an accident and it was nobody's fault, except perhaps, everyone's fault because we do not have a cadre of people continually keeping the markers in the right place when natural things make changes to the scene. Do you understand?"

"Yes Sir. I thank you for explaining it to me," Andy replied, then added, "Can I go now, Sir? I have to help Mac and I don't want to be late to my job."

"That's a good attitude. You are free to go but remember what you learned, it may come in handy someday," Lt. Brown told him.

"I will, Sir. I like what I am learning on the ship," he replied to the Lieutenant.

The Java Sea dropped anchor late that afternoon in an area designated by the harbormaster. Some of the men lowered one of the two lifeboats with the anticipation of going ashore to see the town and visit the harbor side business places for food and miscellaneous personal belongings.

Before they were ready to start the long row into the center of town, a small boat with a jury-rigged sail and three people came within hailing distance of the Java Sea. They introduced themselves as the Physicians Committee of Charleston harbor and advised Captain Murphy and others within hearing distance there would be no one allowed ashore until after a medical inspection the next day. When asked why this was being done they replied, "We have had some fever problems with our citizens and we suspect it came in on a ship. Everyone is being quarantined until we can check them over for signs of the fever. If there is no fever among you, you will be welcome to come ashore. Where did you come from?" they asked.

"We came from Baltimore and this is our first port of call since leaving there four days ago," Captain Murphy informed them.

"I expect you will be cleared. We've not had any Baltimore ships come in with signs of fever. We'll know tomorrow when we check you over. Is there anything of special need you would like sent to you while you are waiting," the man in the bow of their boat asked?

"I don't believe there is as long as you are coming back tomorrow. If our crew has any special needs we can arrange it with you in the morning," Captain Murphy informed him.

"We may not get here in the morning. Our mornings are usually busy. I expect we will get out here closer to 1:30 or 2 in the afternoon. You'll be under quarantine during that time, so just relax and we'll see you tomorrow," he said, with a voice tone and shoulder shrugging to indicate he was the man in charge and there was nothing the Java Sea could do about it.

Standing at the rail with Silas and Mac, Andy said, "That guy has a haughty attitude toward us, doesn't he."

"Some men, when they have a little authority, like to puff themselves up and put everyone on the defensive," Mac told him.

"Yeah, and he's one of them," Silas said. "What he needs is a good bloody nose," he added.

The three of them laughed a little at Silas' last assessment, until that is, Mac said, "As long as we're not going ashore to have dinner in a road house, you and I had better get busy in the galley, Andy my boy."

In the galley, Andy prepared some vegetables for a stew and was working on setting the tables with plates and cups when Captain Murphy came in and asked Andy to go find Silas and bring him down here because the Captain wants to talk with him.

"I think he's up forward in the sail locker, I'll look there first, Captain Murphy," Andy said as he headed for the galley door.

When Andy got back, following about two steps behind Silas, the Captain was sitting at one of the tables with Lt. Brown discussing the inspection they would have to go through tomorrow when the Physicians Committee came again. Silas walked over and sat down with them. Mac looked out through the galley door and asked if they all wanted coffee. When they all said they would, Andy was told to bring it to them.

After the coffee was served, Captain Murphy told Andy to come sit at the table with them so he could learn about the planning of a work project they would schedule tomorrow while waiting for the Committee to come aboard. Andy took a seat across from Lt. Brown and next to Silas who told him, "This will be a good chance to learn something most cabin boys don't learn until their fourth or fifth year on the job. You'll be able to get your Masters and Mates sailing licenses by the time you've reached your seventeenth birthday. Good for you Andy."

Once the coffee was finished Andy cleared the table and the Captain started to explain how he was going to schedule some maintenance work on this voyage. "I'd like to come back with all the masts and spars varnished and a new coat of paint on everything above the waterline and main deck. I think tomorrow will be a good day to tackle the mizzen mast. If we put a good man on the mast in a bo's'n's chair and two men on each spar, they should be able to time their painting in such a way they all work downward and reach the deck at about the same time. What do you think?"

"Won't the wet varnish get all scarred up when we use the sails to get to the dock later in the day?" Asked Lt. Brown.

"It isn't far to the dock and we can get there with the other two masts and the jib sails," Captain Murphy told him, then adding, "We'll be at the dock a couple of days and in this South Carolina temperature the varnish should be well dried before we have to use the mizzen mast sails."

"Now I understand," the Lieutenant said, "If you're not going to use that mast for about three or four days it should work out fine. That's good planning, Captain. I think, by the time this voyage is over I'll be glad I signed on your ship to upgrade my licenses."

"Thank you, Lieutenant Brown. I'll try to teach you some of the tricks of being a Captain on a vessel like this, using my fifteen years experience as a Officer and Captain on several vessels I signed on, over the years, as my guide."

Early the next morning Silas got his crew together to varnish the mizzen mast. Because breakfast was prepared early, Mac let Andy get involved with Silas and the men assigned to do the work. His first job was to help spread out some old sails under the mast so varnish drips wouldn't get on the hatch covers, rails and railings leading to the Captain's quarters.

When the three painters went up the mast to start the work, Andy was given a couple of rags to wipe up drips and told it would be his job to fill the paint buckets when one of the three lowered his bucket for more varnish.

"Only fill the buckets about half full, just in case one is accidentally spilled," Silas said. "We have to use the utmost care. We don't want a big spill on the deck."

Willie Wispor agreed to swing from the Bo's'n's chair and do the mast while Rosco Quinn and Ed Smith painted the yardarms, working from the footropes with a safety line tied to the footrope above. The painters worked fast and Andy found he had plenty of drips to wipe up including some that hit him on the arms, shoulders and back. Silas had loaned him an old hat to keep drips off his head. Every time he wiped up one drip there seemed to be two to take its place. It was a busy time as the three working above painted. The drips got ahead of him when he had to stop and send more paint up to one of them. He discovered if a drip had landed more than fifteen minutes earlier, it would require some scraping to get it off the ship's rails.

The job was finished just before the noon meal and while Andy continued to clean up drips, Willie, Rosco and Ed picked up all the tools, varnish and drop cloths. By the time they were done and came around to inspect Andy's cleanup work, they were satisfied he did a good job except where a few drops had landed on belaying pins in the taff rail. All three told him he had done as good a job as a grown man would have done, which made him feel proud of himself for doing a job the other crewmen complimented him about.

Willie Wispor suggested they let the drips on a few belaying pins harden and scrape them off tomorrow. Ed and Rosco agreed. They told Andy he could scrape them off during his free time after breakfast in the morning.

CHAPTER 10

▼

It was just before two o'clock when the Harbor Master and his assistants came out to the Java Sea and wanted to speak to the Captain and other officers responsible for medical conditions of the crew. Silas was standing gangway watch and called Andy to go summons Captain Murphy and Lieutenant Brown to the gangway to talk to the Harbor Master and his assistants. Lieutenant Brown was on the fo'c'stle talking to some new members of the crew about what their jobs would be as the Java Sea tied up to the dock. He was assuring himself the new men understood how much tension could be placed on the mooring lines without damaging the ship or the dock. Big ships had been known to pull the pilings away from the dock because their crew snubbed off before the ship's forward movement was slowed enough.

Captain Murphy was in his cabin going over the cargo manifest to make sure he understood exactly what was to be unloaded and what was to be loaded here in Charleston. When Andy told him the Harbor Master and his assistants had arrived and wanted to talk to him he said, "It's about time they got here. We're going to be pressed for time to get into the dock today. I hope they're quick about it."

"Come along with me and you can listen and see how these Harbor Masters use their authority," Captain Murphy told him.

Andy tagged along behind the Captain and Lieutenant Brown until they arrived at the gangway rail. He then moved to one side next to Silas where he had a better view of the Harbor Master and his assistants. He looked them over and decided they were not what he believed they should look like for an official of the state who greeted visiting ships.

Captain Murphy spoke first. "I am Captain Fred Murphy. This is my First Officer, Lieutenant Joel Brown. Standing here with us is my Bo's'n, Silas Block and my Cabin boy Andy Murphy. They are here to observe as a training lesson for Andy who is studying to be an officer. This is his first voyage. Shall we get on with the business you are here to conduct?"

"Sure Captain, I'd like to get this over as soon as possible. I'm Captain Rolph a retired mariner from the Grand Banks fishing fleet. This is Doctor Lonson who will inspect your crew and ask a few questions. Would you have your crew come to the main deck and line up for inspection? Doctor Lonson has his associates with him to assist in the survey of the crew so everything should proceed very quickly. We will also need samples of your food to check what the crew, and of course yourself and the other officers, have been eating since you left port in Baltimore. We will take some of the food for testing. Sizeable samples will be needed because our testing entails many steps to check for all the possible fever germs we are confronted with."

Captain Rolph and Dr. Lonson came aboard the Java Sea, followed by four of the doctor's assistants. They went to the main deck and started checking the crew. They were finished in less than five minutes and came back to the head of the gangway where they did the same quick check of the remaining members who were with Captain Murphy.

Captain Rolph's attitude suddenly changed after the inspection was complete. He said, "Now Captain Murphy, we will ask you to produce the food for us that you said you had aboard for your own use. You have a healthy crew and it shouldn't take them long to get it on deck where it can be transferred to the Harbor Master's vessel."

Captain Murphy was well aware of this shakedown and told Silas to furnish two hams, two bags of flour, one bag of coffee and three salt cod.

Captain Rolph immediately asked Dr. Lonson if the list given by Captain Murphy would be enough, to which the doctor answered, "I believe it is only half enough to accomplish our work and suggest the amount be doubled."

Captain Murphy told him, "I'll add one more salt cod, plus one more bag of flour and that's it."

Captain Rolph stepped a little closer to Captain Murphy and in a threatening voice said, "I'm a servant of the local government and you must give us what we need. Now tell your men to double the order."

"You listen to me you old has been. You are using this disguise of yours to raid merchantmen coming to this port on business. I refuse to give you more than we can afford. I must maintain enough for my crew on this voyage. You take what I offered or you won't get anything."

The crew of the Java Sea moved a little closer to be in position if a confrontation should take place between the two captains.

Rolph puffed himself up and said, "Captain Murphy, as a servant and representative of the government hereabouts I will take what I am pleased to take from you rich merchantmen sailing our waters."

With that Captain Murphy reached around the side of the taffrail and produced a double barreled scattergun, saying, "Now you listen to me you thief, I told you what I'd give you and you've worked it into nothing. You get off my ship. I've got to get underway to make the dock before dark."

As old Captain Rolph started to contemplate another move, Lt. Brown blew a short tweeting sound on a small whistle. As Rolph turned around to face the crew, every man pulled a pistol from under his shirt and pointed it straight at him. "Don't shoot, we're leaving," were his last words as he and his crewmates walked off the Java Sea in a different spirit than when they came aboard, ready to pull off another heist from an innocent merchantman. They were beaten.

The thieves just made it back to their own vessel when word went out to hoist the jibs and put all canvas on the main and fore masts. "We've got three miles to go with only a little more than two hours of daylight left and a measly weak breeze at best. The only thing favoring us is the tide," Silas said.

As the Java Sea began to make a little headway toward the Charleston dock, Andy went down to the galley to help Mac start the evening meal. Mac greeted him with, "Hey, you're just in time. I was planning to set the tables and now that you are here you can do it and I'll get busy cutting up some meat. I can boil a few potatoes to go with the ones we had left over at noon. Mashed up together they'll be all right. Once the tables are set up, you can go into the stores and bring me some cabbage to fry. We'll be ready by the time we make the dock."

"Should I take the Captain a cup of coffee now that we are beginning to move to the dock," Andy asked?

"That's a good idea. I'll make a fresh pot while you are setting tables and then I'll cut the meat. By the time you are back with the cabbage, the coffee will be ready. Captain Murphy will appreciate a fresh cup of coffee this time of day, especially after the delay caused by the fake Harbor Master and his ruffians."

As Andy walked topside with the Captain's coffee and headed aft toward his cabin, he noticed all the sails were set on the fore and main masts, and all but one jib had been raised. He could feel a little breeze against his face. It was not enough to cause the big sails to billow, which meant only the sky sails and royals were doing any work to move the ship closer to the dock. He realized they might eat their meal while they were sailing to the dock and some of the men might have to leave the meal to rush up the masts to lower the sails, leaving their food half eaten. If that happened he and Mac would have to reheat each man's food when he finished his docking chores.

This was a new realization for Andy. The work on a ship must come before crew comforts when the ship is coming or leaving port. Control of the ship must be maintained at all times. Docking was no easy thing. It took coordination of many hands.

When Andy walked into Captain Murphy's cabin with the fresh coffee, the Captain said, "I smell coffee. It's just what I need. You and Mac sure know how to take good care of the necessary needs of the old man. You be sure and thank him for me."

"Yes Sir, Captain Murphy. Is there anything else you need right now? We're just getting started on the night meal which will probably be served while we're on the way to the dock."

"I think not, Andy but I would like you to come see me when you have finished your work for the day and the night meal is cleared away. I'd like to get your opinion and understanding of what happened this afternoon."

By the time the meal was finished and Andy got back to the main deck he could see the dock only a few yards away. There were fewer sails and jibs up now. The Java Sea was easing into the dock, her starboard side rigged with the large hawsers she would be tied up with. He watched as Ed Smith and Rosco Quinn threw the heaving lines onto the dock so line handlers could pull the hawsers over and make the ship fast to the pilings. It was the first time he had seen a ship tied up while he was on the deck watching. There was a lot of squealing and groaning coming from the pilings and the hawsers as the ship came to a halt.

Andy walked down to the mess hall and picked up a broom to sweep around the tables as Mac came out of the galley into the dinning area. He was holding two cups of coffee and said to Andy, "Hey, Andy you can let that sweeping go and I will do it after Silas and I have our coffee. We don't need you stirring up any dust, the coffee tastes bad enough as comes from the pot."

"Captain Murphy wants to see me as soon as I am finished with my work. Shall I take him a cup of coffee, too?"

"This coffee is getting a bit strong because it has set in the pot for a couple of hours. If you come back in an hour, I'll have a fresh pot and the Captain can have the first cup. I'll save the rest for the night watch. Tied to the dock there will be more men on watch overnight. There will also be a deck patrol to prevent thieves from sneaking aboard and making off with our stores."

Andy knocked on the Captain's door and entered. He said, "Captain Murphy, I am back to talk to you about the Harbor Master thing this afternoon."

"Good, Andy. Lieutenant Brown and I were just discussing our projected stay here in Charleston. If all goes well we should be leaving here the day after tomorrow if there is no additional cargo to load. As it stands right now, we have to off-load some farming tools, maple lumber and those five big boxes of furniture. We will be using the space for farm produce like carrots, beets, potatoes and winter squash. All of those things will keep until we get to Trinidad and other South America ports. By the time we get to the southern end of our cruise, it will be winter down there and the vegetables will fare better."

Lieutenant Brown spoke up and told him, "Andy, you are a very fortunate young man to be serving as a cabin boy and included in the discussions, planning and decision making involved in the overall ship operations."

"Yes, Sir, I know it and appreciate Captain Murphy giving me the extra training on my first cruise."

Captain Murphy spoke up and informed them he always tried to teach his cabin boys everything they might need to know if they became long-term sailors, or just made one cruise. "Jimmy Mixon, who you know, was my last cabin boy. He became trained enough, after a few trips to get his officer's papers and can always go to sea to make a good living for his family. Although it seems he is now becoming a landlubber with dreams of farming on the land just north of the Annapolis area. I wish him well."

"I'd like to change the subject to the Harbor Master and his medical team who inspected us this afternoon, while it is fresh in our memories. First off, I have been keeping it a secret, but in a couple of ports, when I met with Captains of other ships, they informed me of the inspections being done in Charleston by a purported Harbor Master and a Doctor.

"I was given the names Rolph and Lonson. I didn't remember it yesterday when they first approached us but after they left I looked up the information I had written in my personal log. Sure enough Rolph and Lonson were the names I had been given by the other Captains.

"Once I knew we were being hijacked, I had Silas arm the crew in preparation of a showdown when they returned. Silas, Lt. Brown and I worked it out in my quarters while everyone was busy with the mast painting and other ship work yesterday morning. Everyone did a good job and we were able to fend them off, putting them in their place at the same time. I'll call an assembly of the crew when we get back to sea and thank all of them for their part in saving the Java Sea from the riffraff."

Looking toward Andy, Lt Brown said, "I'm sure the men will enjoy being acknowledged for their part and it will help boost their spirit on a long cruise to know they are appreciated. It will give us something to talk to them about as we continue into the southern waters. As the navigator and person who gave the sounding blast to go into action I feel the crew did a very good job of it."

Captain Murphy directed his attention to Andy and said, "There are a lot of fakers out here on the open seas and some in the harbors. They are ready to steal anything they can get away with. Captain Rolph and his cohort Dr. Lonson are thieves, and if I hadn't been forewarned by other captains, they would have been able to pull the same trick on us they are pulling on other ships coming into port here. They were really trying to get some of our food without having to do anything to earn it. I hope we have all learned a lesson from this and keep ourselves aware of whom we are confronting when the Java Sea may be in jeopardy."

"You certainly did a good job in preparing for a confrontation and had your crew well informed to overcome them. I congratulate you Captain Murphy on your skills and leadership. It is a pleasure to sail with you, Sir," Lt. Brown said.

"Yeah, me too," Andy added.

Both officers chuckled at the young cabin boy's input at the end of the discussion. They realized Andy hadn't said a word during the discussion and his boyish remark, agreeing with Lt. Brown at least let them know he was happy with the outcome too.

"That's all for tonight, Andy. You can go do whatever you want and I'll see you when you bring my morning coffee. Good night."

"Thank you, Captain Murphy. Before I go, Mac said he would have a fresh pot of coffee ready when we were through and if you and Lt. Brown would like some I'll bring back two cups before I quit for the night."

"What do you think about a fresh cup of coffee, Joel," Captain Murphy asked?

"I'd say it is a good idea," he replied.

"I'll be right back," Andy said as he headed for the door to get the coffee for a couple of officers he was beginning to admire more all the time. They were two thoughtful and alert teachers, helping a cabin boy learn about the ways of the sea on his first voyage.

The Java Sea's crew was up early the next morning. Mac and Andy had breakfast ready before 5:30 and most of the crew had eaten and left the tables to begin their unloading work by the time the sun came up at 6:15. Only a few lingering over a second cup of coffee, with sleep still in their eyes, were eating the last of their food. Andy worked around them as he cleared tables, loaded the garbage buckets, carried dishes into the galley to be washed and refilled the salt and pepper shakers which were secured to the table tops.

Andy's time helping Mac seemed to pass more quickly on the mornings he was busy and this had been one of them. Before 9am he went topside and watched the crew load the last of the vegetables consigned to Port of Spain, Trinidad. It would be the next stop for the Java Sea.

Andy went to the galley about 11am to help Mac with the noon meal. He was told to go back on deck and watch the crew work the ship away from the dock. "I think you will find it interesting, Mac told him. The crew will manually pull her around with a lifeboat and hawsers attached to the dock. It is a bit of seamanship you should learn about."

Mac was right as usual. Andy watched from the wheel deck as six men in a lifeboat rowed hard to pull the bow away from the dock and swing the vessel broadside the harbor. Meanwhile two men attended the mooring hawsers eased them off as the ship swung around in answer to the tow from the lifeboat. Once the Java Sea was swung crosswise the harbor the lifeboat and its crew picked up the line handlers from the dock. They were all hoisted aboard, where they immediately climbed the main and mizzen masts to release the lower sails.

For a few moments the big ship just sat there floating like she was asleep. Then a slight breeze began to catch in the sky sails and royals. She slowly came to life and began to move toward the open sea. Soon, passing a point of land that jutted out from the mainland coast, her large sails filled and she was on her way to Trinidad.

Andy went back to the galley, excitement filling his mind as he hurriedly explained to Mac how the crew had moved the ship to where she could sail away on her own without danger of running aground in the harbor.

Mac's reaction to Andy was, "I thought you'd find it interesting. Now we have to finish up this meal. We're going to have a crew to feed in about fifteen minutes and with this late lunch they'll be rambunctious to eat."

"OK, Mac I'll get hard at it. I want to thank you for giving me the time off to see the undocking."

"You have to learn, kid. You have to learn. That's what Captain Murphy wants for you. I just try to help."

CHAPTER 11

▼

The first two days out of Charleston were uneventful, routine days. Andy got to see a lot of ocean and wondered how big it would be if all the oceans and seas were combined. He asked Mac and Silas how big all the seas and oceans were if they were combined and was told he should ask the navigator Lt. Brown. "He's the one with all the charts and knowledge of the sizes of the many oceans and seas," Silas remarked.

With his curiosity aroused and his work at a lull point, he went looking for Lt. Brown. He found him taking readings on an island that was just beginning to show itself above the horizon off the starboard bow. "Lieutenant Brown, Sir, I asked Mac and Silas how big all the oceans and seas were and they said I should ask you because you would have that kind of information."

"Wow, Andy I never figured it out and I'm not sure my charts have enough information on them so I could figure it out, if I had the time. The Atlantic and Pacific oceans alone are about one hundred million square miles. By the time you add the smaller oceans and the seas, you will have at least another fifty million square miles. So, two hundred and fifty million square miles is not a bad guess. If I can find all the figures I'll give them to you and you can add them together and figure it out for yourself. It would be good practice for you, working with the figures and you'll get a good idea of how vast the oceans and seas are on the earth."

"Thank you," Lieutenant Brown, Sir"

"If you are not very busy now, would you like to watch me figure out how far away that island is we see on the horizon?

"Yes sir."

"You can even help if you would like. First, do you see that cross marked on the deck?"

"Yes sir."

"There is another one back aft. As soon as we get an angle measurement from here we will rush back to the aft marker and get the angle from it. I know the distance between the two markers and we can figure the distance to the island using a mathematical formula for triangulation. What I would like you to do is lock the compass when I say 'Mark'."

Lt. Brown showed Andy how to lock the compass needle on the bearing when he was satisfied he had a good bearing on a spot he would be able to pick up in his glass from the aft marker. Andy took the compass and held it as Lt. Brown instructed him. Lt. Brown put the glass into a bracket on the side of the compass especially made to hold both instruments in line with each other. At the word Mark, Andy pushed the little locking button down and the needle stopped any slight movement it was making.

They went back to the after marker and did the procedure again. When Lt. Brown had written down all the compass angles, he told Andy they were going to do it all over again, only this time they would take the after reading first. They were soon finished and Lt. Brown put the compass and glass back in the case for safe keeping.

"I am going down to the chart table to do the figuring. If you are still free you can come along and see how it is worked out," he told Andy.

"I better check with Mac first. I've been away quite a while. If he doesn't need me I'll be right back. Would you like some coffee?"

"That's a great idea to go along with the pencil work I will be doing on these figures," Lt. Brown said.

When Andy arrived in the galley there were four crewmen gathered around Silas as he explained what the offloading would be like in Trinidad. "We may be picking up some cargo and if so the procedures will be just the reverse of the unloading. Ed Smith, Rosco Quinn and Willie Wispor are all familiar with the Java Sea's cargo handling systems, so I advise all of you new crewmen to do it the way they tell you, so no one gets hurt."

Mac came out of the galley and asked Andy where he had been all afternoon. Andy told him he was learning triangulation to an island from Lt. Brown and if he wasn't needed he was going to take coffee to Captain Murphy and Lt. Brown.

"Lt. Brown is going to teach me how to figure distances with a compass and a known triangle base line." He told Mac.

When the others overheard the conversation, they all started teasing Andy and making remarks like: "The kid is going to get an education from the Lieutenant." "He'll run us up on a ledge somewhere if he listens to Mr. Brown." "How do you expect us to be fed if Mac doesn't have you to show him what to do?" "Kid, I'll tell ya, you have to go by the color of the water to tell where you're going." They all laughed at their teasing except Andy.

Andy said, "The color of the water doesn't help. The water today is a different color than it was yesterday and it is becoming more of a light blue every day. When we left Baltimore it was a darker greenish color."

Silas laid back and let a big roaring laugh out of his deep bass throat. "The kid has you cornered this time," he told the hecklers, adding, "Nice going Andy. It shows you are being observant and learning some things on your own."

Mac stepped out of the galley and said, "You guys better watch out for this kid, he's been to school and can outsmart all of us without schooling, except what we picked up on a sailing vessel, or perhaps a couple of grades when we were about five or six years old."

Andy went into the galley and picked up two cups to fill with coffee for Captain Murphy and Lieutenant Brown. Mac had made a fresh pot while he was being heckled, so he waited a few minutes for it to finish cooking. He thought about what the men had said and wondered if he was cut out for a sailor's life, even though it had been his dream since he was a small boy.

Mac walked in and told him he needed to put on his toughest skin or the crew would keep heckling him. "They enjoy it. Sometimes I think they are a little envious of your age and status as cabin boy. They'd like that job but are too old for it, so they heckle the guy who has it. You shouldn't worry about it. Most of them including some of the hecklers have told me they like you and think you are a good example of what a cabin boy should be."

Andy thanked Mac for the words of praise. He picked up the two cups of coffee and headed for the chart room to get his lesson from Lieutenant Brown.

"Am I glad to see you back with the coffee? I can use it about now to settle my stomach down from the acidity that developed after lunch. I have all the tables laid out ready to figure how far the island is from our course. The tables have all the specific sine and cosines we will need to figure out the problem with the angles we made with the compass. By the way, did you have any math and trigonometry in school?" Lt. Brown inquired.

"I had some geometry and was just starting trigonometry when I left to go on the Java Sea as cabin boy." Andy replied.

Lt. Joel Brown proved to have the patience of Job in teaching Andy the neces-sary math he would need to learn navigation. And, Andy was an attentive pupil. He was smart and picked up the 'tricks of the trade' easily. The two of them worked together most of the time when there was any positioning to figure. Within a month, Andy was taking the sightings, figuring the position and Lt. Brown was checking his figures. The Lt. seldom found an error in Andy's work.

Navigation became a second job for Andy whenever all his other work, with Mac and Silas, was not pressing. He enjoyed working with Lt. Brown because of the friendly temperament of the navigator.

Mac and Silas always made time for him to work with them and others when there was a job being done he needed to learn. He was getting the best of the best in his training.

Two days before they pulled into Trinidad he was working with Silas one morning and right out of the blue, Silas said, "OK kid, you're going to climb the mast and I'll give you twenty seconds to make the top of the main mast."

"Wow," Andy exclaimed. "I haven't climbed before and I don't know if I can do it that fast."

"Well, in an emergency you might have to go up that fast or faster. If there is a man up there who lost his footrope and has fallen, with his leg pinned between a shroud and the mast, it might be necessary to run up the mast to save him," Silas said, posing a hypothetical problem for him to think about.

"Now, let's get back to reality. You could fall and be killed on your first climb if you try to set a climbing record while going up a mast. Your first lesson is how to get from the deck onto the shrouds to start climbing. Come over here by the rail and I will show you the best and safest procedure for getting onto the shrouds from the deck.

"The first lesson is one I want you to learn and always practice whenever you go aloft on this or any other ship. It is the rule: 'One hand for the ship and one hand for your self.' I want you to remember that and do it when you climb. Climbing is the most serious business you will ever do on a sailing vessel and your life is in your own hands. Never get smart or reckless. Do you understand that?"

"Yes, Silas, I sure do." Andy replied to the question because he knew Silas was very serious about teaching him the right way to climb in the rigging.

"OK, I'll show you how to mount the bottom rung of the shrouds and then you can try it. First you reach up with your hand and grab the shrouds about right here, you swing your opposite side foot up onto the belaying rack. Bring your other foot onto the rack and step up on the bottom line of the shroud ladder. Now grasp the ladder rungs with your free hand. Do you see how I am doing it?"

"Yes. I think I can do it."

"Good. You try it and I'll watch you have the right ease of movement. Do not attempt to climb. I only want you to learn how to start climbing. We need to practice that first until you can do it blindfolded."

After several tries at mounting and dismounting the shrouds, Silas told him, "You seem to have a natural knack for swinging yourself up and around the shrouds. We'll try this again one of these days and then I'll teach you to climb. I don't want you to do this if I am not with you to make sure you are doing it right. Understand?"

Andy gave him an affirmative reply and at the same time Mac yelled out the galley door, "Where's Andy? I need him."

As Andy walked into the galley, Mac said, "I'm way behind in my work. I need you to peel those potatoes and cut the tops off the carrots."

"Don't get yourself overloaded in the work because I am training in seamanship. You should always call me. This work comes first for me and I need to learn what it takes to prepare the meals and keep the galley running on time," Andy told him.

Andy put on an apron, picked up a knife, and started to peel potatoes. Except for the banging of a few pots and pans, Mac was silent as the two worked together in the small galley spaces. Andy had peeled about 8 of the potatoes when Mac moved closer to him to work on the butcher block. He was cutting and trimming some of the last of the beef they had picked up in Charleston.

"I know your cabin boy work comes first and I have been overworking myself to give you more time for seamanship lessons, but I am going to have to call on you for more help because I just can't handle the job all the time by myself. I apologize for getting kind of gruff when you returned. I was just feeling like I couldn't see the end of this meal."

"That's OK, Mac. I understand how tough it gets putting a big meal together for the crew and the officers. I've already learned it is a tough job and when we are at sea, with people eating at different times, because of other ship's work, it must be a lot harder to keep up. I didn't expect an apology. It's accepted, and Thank You for it, if you think it is needed," Andy told him, using the easy, humble manner his parents had instilled in him.

"Well, Thank You, Andy. With an attitude like yours we will have no trouble getting along and the work will get done. You're a good boy. I'm glad you got the cabin boy job," Mac assured him.

CHAPTER 12

▼

Six days later the Java Sea anchored in the harbor at Port of Spain, Trinidad. Two lifeboats were lowered and Captain Murphy went ashore to make arrangements for someone to come out to the anchorage to pick up the cargo to be unloaded for a variety of Trinidad customers.

When Andy asked Silas why they didn't tie up to the dock like they did in Charleston, he explained it was because of the size of the cargo being off loaded. The dock in Port of Spain is too narrow to take the oversized boxes of tools the Java Sea is leaving here.

"They will have to come out to the anchorage with a barge of some kind and we will offload onto it using the main mast yardarm as a boom. When they arrive, I will make sure you have some free time to watch the operations. It will teach you how a ship can handle big, bulky cargo when there is no wharf crane available. Participation and observation of an offloading onto a barge will look good on your seamanship examination papers."

Andy went back to the galley, thinking of what Silas had said about the unloading onto a barge and his promise to have him as an observer which would benefit his seaman rating in the future. He was happy to think he would have a part in it even as an onlooker.

As soon as he stepped into the galley, Mac directed him to sit down at one of the tables because he wanted to talk to him a few minutes. Andy chose the table nearest the hatch leading to the main deck where a slight breeze was blowing in and it was a little cooler than the rest of the chow hall. Mac came and sat down across the table from him.

"Andy, Silas has been telling me you are beginning to get the hang of climbing the shrouds and ratlines. He said you are able to swing yourself up to the first rat-lines in one smooth motion now, and he is going to start you climbing higher sometime next week.

"Andy, climbing on a ship is a dangerous job. I was a climber when I was a lot younger than I am now. Climbers, if they are good at it, and do the high work on the sky sails and royals, make better pay than an ordinary seaman who only climbs to the first two yardarms.

"I was a high man. One day I was working down low on the main yardarm. We were putting on studding sails and running out the studding yards to take advantage of a nice breeze that was holding steady. We were on a starboard tack so the ship was leaning to starboard. I was working on the port side right over the port rail. I had been leaning over the yardarm and was tying off the inboard end of the studding yard when the footrope broke without warning. I had no safety rope and was not hanging on because I felt secure working at the lower level while standing on a footrope. I fell, striking my hip and thigh over the rail. I passed out from the pain.

"The crew picked me up and put me in a bunk. We had one man who served as the doctor. He had been to college and had studied some medical type courses. He told the ship's carpenter how to make some splints for my leg because he thought it might be broken. I couldn't walk for three weeks and when I did walk it was painful. The cabin boy and a couple of others took care of me until I could manage on my own.

"The reason I am a ship's cook today is because I was never able to climb again. My hip and knee won't bend enough to climb the ropes."

"Gee, I'm sorry, Mac," Andy sympathized.

"Silas is a good teacher and will watch over you like a mother hen watches over her chicks. The end results are dependent on you and what I am trying to instill in you is, you are going to have to be responsible for yourself when you're aloft. You have to watch the equipment, the weather, the movement of the ship and you must always use one hand to hang on for safety's sake. We like you kid and no one in the whole crew wants to see you get hurt if we can do anything to prevent it."

"Golly, that is very thoughtful of you Mac. I appreciate your telling me the crew thinks of my safety, as I learn to be a cabin boy and sailor. I feel grateful for the support I am getting as I learn."

"Say, Kid. How much schooling did you have before you quit?"

"We had a one-room schoolhouse on the Annapolis Road. Most years it had six grades. I started there when I was five and graduated from the sixth grade when I was nearly twelve. My first teacher was a Miss Collamore and my last teacher was my sister Maria. Going to school in a one room schoolhouse means you hear the same six grades every year. What you don't get one year, you can hear it again the next year as the class behind you studies the same subjects. I think it works out well for students because they are always reviewing the previous years. Plus, with my older sister being the teacher I got a lot of help at home on things I had a little trouble learning. Does that explain what you are interested in knowing about my education?"

"I knew there was a reason you were smarter than most kids who come from schools in the big towns and cities. You seem to take an interest and do things without being told. You know how to do things without someone standing beside you instructing every move." Mac told him.

"I learned a lot of things working on the farm that were similar to the duties on the ship. That makes it easier, too," Andy said.

"Our chat has gone on long enough. We have a meal to do. Go check on the Captain and Lieutenant to see what they may need and I'll start on the cooking end of the job," Mac said.

Andy headed up the ladder to the main deck and into the fresh air. As he walked back aft to the cabins he thought over what Mac had been saying about him and his education. He realized he did understand a lot of things other twelve-year-old boys didn't understand. It was then he realized his family back home on the farm outside of Baltimore was the reason. We were a close knit family who always worked together for the benefit of each other. We were like the old story of friends who had a slogan of 'one for all and all for one.' He began to appreciate home a little more as he thought.

Entering the cabin, he found Lt. Brown working on some navigational charts and Captain Murphy going over the cargo lists for Trinidad. The Captain looked up and said, "Well, now if it isn't my favorite cabin boy. How long before the cooking will be finished so I won't starve on this voyage?" he joked.

"Mac and I are both tired so we've decided not to feed again until tomorrow," Andy joked back.

"Oh, oh, the cabin boy has been spending too much time with Silas and Mac. He is beginning to sound just like them." Captain Murphy said, with a little laugh at his own joke.

"I believe the meal will be served within the hour. I came here to find out if you wanted to eat in the chow hall or your quarters," Andy asked?

"I'll come down to the chow hall," Captain Murphy said. "I want to talk to some of the men about our offloading those big machinery boxes in Port of Spain."

"That's good for me, too," added Lt. Brown.

"Would either of you like coffee or cold tea while you wait?" Andy asked.

With a yes reply from both men for cold tea, he turned and started for the door. Once out on the deck he thought about how he joked back when the Captain and Lt. Brown had remarked about being hungry. He realized they joked back and forth with him, but he was still unsure if he should joke back to them. He decided to ask Mac as soon as he was finished with the present workload, which had to be completed, before anything else could be started.

As Andy walked into the chow hall on his way to the galley to get the cold tea for the officers, he noticed Silas sitting at one of the tables. Silas said, "I don't want you practicing to mount the shrouds and ratlines with your left hand as Willie Wispor suggested to you. Willie explained to me about his talk and instructions to you. You'll be better off if you ignore what he said because Willie is a very ambidextrous individual who believes everyone can work with both hands as easily as he does. Although you work well with your left hand, you are predominantly right handed and it is your strongest hand when you work. That's the hand you should use to mount the rigging. I won't keep you, I know you're busy nearing mealtime, but I want you to do it my way while you are learning."

"I agree with you the right hand is my strongest. I will feel better doing it with my right hand. Maybe someday I can use either hand when I get older and stronger."

"That's the right way to look at it. I think Willie already understands. Now you better get on with your duties or we'll have Mac come out here on a rampage, after us with his meat cleaver."

When Andy went into the galley Mac was sputtering about getting the ship underway to make the vents bring in some air. Andy said, "I didn't understand what you said as I came in the door because of the noise behind me in the chow hall."

Andy explained to Mac he was going to take some cool tea to the officers and would then be ready to help him with the cooking. "They already told me they would be eating in the chow hall, so we don't have to prepare trays for them."

"I was just doing my usual ranting and raving when I talk to myself. It is so hot in this galley I would like to get underway so we could have a little air coming in through the vents," he told Andy.

"Isn't there anything we can do to bring air in through the vents when we are tied up or anchored?" asked Andy.

"No, there has to be a movement of air coming in through the vents and that only happens when the ship is underway or there is a good breeze blowing and the vent cowling can be pointed into it," Mac replied.

"I'll have to have Silas tell me about how the ventilation works and maybe we can work something out to get a vent down here when it is hot like today," Andy told him.

"We'd be better off to get the cooking finished and the meal on the tables so we can get out of this hotbox," Mac said.

"I'll figure out something to get the heat out of here, or my name isn't Andy Thomas Murphy and I'm not Irish," he said with a chuckle.

He and Mac had been working on the meal as they talked, with an end result of having it nearly complete. They both got busy cutting up some clean salad vegetables they had purchased from a farmer on the outskirts of town. At least they would be cool and appetizing when compared to the hot food Mac had been preparing. Andy took the large bowls of salad into the chow hall as Mac dished up the meat and hot vegetables into several large crocks. Andy carried the heaviest of the bowls into the chow hall as Mac pulled on the rope attached to the diner bell, ringing it loudly for all to hear.

As the crew members began to show up for the suppertime meal, Ed Smith came in and announced the barge was tied up along side the Java Sea. He said there were five men in each of the two boats acting as tugs to the barge. With four rowers in each boat they were able to move the empty barge easily through the harbor. He said he estimated the barge to be twenty feet wide by at least twenty-five feet long.

When Ed had finished talking and sat down next to Rosco Quinn and Willie Wispor, Silas came down the ladder to the chow hall and said the barge was nearly finished with tying up to the Java Sea. They dropped an anchor about 50 yards off our starboard beam and rowed a couple of lines over to tie onto our rail for the night. They built a fire in an old stone fireplace on the far end of the barge and began cooking their supper while they were still tying up.

Looking at Andy, Silas said, "Tell Mac he won't have to feed the barge crew until breakfast. They're cooking their own supper."

The Trinidad barge handlers spent their evening hours talking, singing and dancing. Although the Java Sea's crew didn't understand what they were talking about, they did enjoy the rhythm of their music. It was interesting to watch them drum on just about anything to get a rhythmic sound for their songs. Sometimes they would slap the rhythm of a song on the side of their leg.

At 8:30 pm Andy took some coffee to Captain Murphy and Lieutenant Brown. They both expressed thanks for the pre bedtime drink. Captain Murphy asked Andy if he was going to be involved in off loading of the big boxes.

"Silas said he was going to make sure I was able to watch it all and could stand on the poop deck for a good view of how it will be accomplished."

"That's good. Silas is a good man and is always ahead of the timing in most all of the ship's work. He is often ready ahead of time when work has to be done aboard ship. I am fortunate to have as skilled a bo's'n as Silas on the Java Sea. He takes a lot of worry off of me, I am sure of that," Captain Murphy stated.

As Andy was about to leave, Lt. Brown asked him if he was still enjoying his work on the ship, to which Andy replied, "Yes Sir. I especially like the work we do together with the mathematic formulas and figuring out the triangulation problems that relate to distances from the ship to shore points. It's a lot of work but it is fun work. I always liked arithmetic and mathematics in school."

"It is good that you do, Andy, because life itself is built more and more around some kind of numeric system. I predict the future will be filled with math, and the more you know about the relationships that can be worked out, using numerals the easier it will be to understand varied problems of life."

"Yes sir. Is there anything else either of you want tonight," he asked?

Both officers said, "No."

Captain Murphy said, "We will both eat a late breakfast in the chow hall so as not to interfere with Mac feeding the barge crew in the morning. If all works out well, perhaps we can get underway tomorrow a little after noon. You can bring us a cup of coffee when you get up. Good Night, Andy."

"Good night and thank you Captain Murphy, Sir."

"Good night Lieutenant Brown."

Busy with his charts, Lt. Brown mumbled a low pitched, nearly inaudible, "Good night."

CHAPTER 13

▼

Everyone got up early on the day of the offloading in Port of Spain, Trinidad. Andy's first job was to take coffee to Captain Murphy and Lt. Brown. Mac had made some French toast and sent along a couple of slices for each man with a little orange marmalade for topping. He told Andy, "You can tell them I sent this to keep them alive until they can get into the chow hall for a real breakfast."

Holding the tray in both hands Andy started up to the main deck when he remembered the sugar container in the Captain's quarters was nearly empty and Captain Murphy liked a lot of sugar in his coffee in the morning. He believed he needed the sugar for energy to keep himself alert all day. Returning to the galley he told Mac he needed sugar for the Captain's quarters. "You go on ahead and I'll bring it right up. We don't want their toast and coffee getting cold or we'll be the ones needing energy trying to get away from their whip."

"Yeah, sure," Andy replied, laughing at Mac's humor.

When he walked into the Officers' Quarters, Lt. Brown was standing by the chart table in his robe. Captain Murphy's room door was closed.

Lt. Brown said, "Good Morning, Andy."

He replied, "Good Morning Lieutenant Brown. I have some coffee and French toast for you and Captain Murphy which Mac said would keep you alive until you could get to the chow hall. Mac is coming with the sugar because I didn't have much room on the tray and he didn't want the toast to get cold."

As Andy finished talking Captain Murphy's door opened and he said, "It smells like there's coffee out here in the chart room. Oh, I guess there must be coffee, Andy's here. Good Morning, Andy."

"Good Morning, Captain Murphy, Sir."

"What's going on with the crew at this time of the morning," the Captain asked?

"All of the crew is nearly finished with their food. We have the ten with the barge to feed and the chow hall will be cleaned up as soon as they finish. Then we will set a table for you and Mr. Brown. Is there anything more for either of you now or should I leave and help Mac take care of the barge crew?"

"I think I am satisfied with the coffee and French toast for now. I will see you later when the table is prepared for us. Thank you Andy, and thank Mac for me," Captain Murphy said.

When Andy got back to the galley he found the sugar container sitting on the end of the galley work table. Without saying anything to Mac he took it back to the Officers' Quarters and left it beside the partial container. Returning to the galley he found Mac scurrying around looking for something. Mac said, "I had the sugar container ready and I don't remember where I set it down. Will you find it and take it to the Captain?"

"I did already," Andy told him. "The captain told me to thank you for the French toast."

"Good boy. I should have known you were ahead of me again. If I had put my thinking cap on I would have realized the reason I couldn't find it was because you had gone to deliver it."

Andy looked around to see what had to be worked on and asked Mac if he had anything special to do, or should he start the cleanup in the chow hall. He was told to start the cleanup and work around the three stragglers who were the men coming off the night watch. The regular crew were finished eating and the barge crew would eat as soon as the chow hall was ready to take them. By the time the three stragglers left the chow hall, Andy was nearly ready for the barge crew to come in and eat.

"I made a large kettle of tea for them because they don't drink coffee. We will have to give them a shot of rum in their tea. We must make sure they only have one shot per man. We don't want anyone seeing double while they are working on the cargo. Most of these Port of Spain stevedores are good workers and easy to get along with. Although, like everywhere, when it comes to cargo handlers, there's often one with a belligerent attitude," Mac informed him.

The barge crew sat quietly and ate their meal. When Mac explained there was no more they quietly left the chow hall and went on deck to work on the cargo unloading. Andy and Mac returned to the cleanup, preparing the first table for the Captain and Lieutenant. When it was finished, Mac said, "You can go tell the officers we're ready for them. After we get them out of the way, we can have our own breakfast."

It was now ten minutes before seven and both officers came in to eat at the same time, making Mac and Andy happy they didn't have to wait on one of them coming in later. As soon as they were seated Captain Murphy said, "I'll only have coffee. The French toast and marmalade was enough for a while. I still hope we can get underway around noon time. With a decent breeze we can clear the islands overnight and if any pirates are around we won't have to worry about them seeing us if we stay close to the coast of South America."

Lieutenant Brown asked if it would be much trouble to make him a couple of pieces of toast with some more of that marmalade on them. "I have always liked orange marmalade and this morning it tasted wonderful."

"I'll have it up in a jiffy for you," Mac told him. "Come on Andy, you can make a fresh pot of coffee while I make the toast and get a side dish of marmalade ready for Mr. Brown."

When they returned to the table with fresh coffee and the toast, Captain Murphy invited them to sit down and talk about their feeding of the barge crew.

"Did anything out of the ordinary happen while the stevedores were eating their breakfast?" Captain Murphy asked, directing the question to both Mac and Andy.

"I spent most of the time in the galley and Andy worked the chow hall," Mac replied. "There was some loud talking but I didn't pay attention to it because they always talk loud at the docks in Port of Spain."

"What about you, Andy. Did you think everything went smoothly?"

"The only thing I saw was an argument between two of them over the last piece of toast. A big, burly man walked over to them, cut the toast in half and spoke sternly to them in Spanish. They sat back down, each with a half piece of toast, and all was quiet. I think he was the gang boss or something."

"Thank you, Andy. It sounds like my request for a firm leader to keep the crew in line was adhered to by the docking company. It is a good thing the big man was in their crew to keep peace. Sometimes they get into knife fights over silly things if they don't have a strong leader in charge." Captain Murphy explained.

Around the Caribbean area, sailors on American ships were alert to the fact many of the dock workers carried knives and machetes under their baggy clothing. Ships making port calls in many areas usually warned their crews of the danger of arguing or belittling any of the natives. It seemed to be a way of life with them to reach for a knife at the first sign of a foreigner doing anything they believed was meant to take advantage of them and their friends. They could be wrong but their misunderstanding of a foreigner's ways and language made no difference, they were their own judge and jury, it was their right to make all determinations when dealing with strangers.

Mac and Andy sat with Captain Murphy and Lt. Brown until they finished their coffee and went back to their quarters. They finally sat down to their own breakfast at 7:15. Mac had made some ham, fresh coffee, toast with a side dish of fruit and scrambled a pan of eggs while Andy cleaned the remaining tables and sat places for the two of them.

Once they were seated, Mac said, "You won't get this kind of breakfast every day so enjoy it while you can. These are fresh eggs. I purchased a case from a ship chandler who recognized the Java Sea and brought a dory load along side to sell."

With their meal out of the way, Mac told Andy he could go watch the unloading until 10:30 when he wanted him back to start the noon meal. "If we get unloaded in time for a noontime sailing, you can stay there longer. As soon as I get the word from Silas, I will let you know a time."

As soon as Andy got to the main deck he noticed there were a lot of changes in the rigging on the main mast and the main yardarm was not in the position where it was usually set. He went up on the poop deck where he could get a better look at what was being done to offload the cargo. He had never before seen a yardarm used as a boom for handling cargo as big as what was coming out of number two hold. The box was at least eight feet square by five feet deep. It had been slung with ropes and was being lifted to the tip of the main yardarm with ropes and pulleys which were called block and tackle aboard ships.

Once the box was high up against the tip of the yardarm on the starboard side, Silas called out through a megaphone he was carrying to cease hoisting. The order was then given to swing the box out over the side where it could be lowered to the barge. To swing the box out there was a running line which allowed the yardarm to extend over the side of the ship further than its normal position. It was then lowered and the box was set on large blocks of wood so the ropes it was tied with could be untied and pulled from beneath the box.

The stevedores working on the barge lifted the box with levers and placed rollers under it so they could move it to a different position on the barge. By the time they had finished the first box, the second one was about to be lowered to the barge. Using the same procedure, the ship's crew put the boxes aboard the barge nearly as fast as the barge crew could put them in the position where they moved them. It was a fast operation and each box seemed to move along a little faster than the one before.

Next were the large tool and equipment boxes. At least five feet square on their ends with a length of sixteen and eighteen feet each, Andy didn't see how they could handle such outsized boxes. His answer came from Silas when he came down from the fo'c'sle and told the crew how to double rig the boxes with a single rope going around one end then to the center making a loop. Go around the other end, back to the center with a matching loop and then around the original end. This gave a double strand to carry the load.

As the long boxes came out of the hold, they were lifted to a position standing on end. They were then lifted out and laid across the hatch where they changed the point of lift to the center loops Silas had rigged on the boxes. Next they were lifted and laid flat on the barge. They were moved into position on rollers keeping the barge floating level. The heavy boxes would have tilted the barge too much if they were not positioned properly.

Once the offloading was completed, Silas had the crew work on restoring the rigging to its normal settings. Andy was sent to tell the Captain the cargo had been unloaded and within the hour the Java Sea would be ready to sail from the Port of Spain.

Captain Murphy was pleased with the news and said to tell Mac he would eat an early lunch because he wanted to take the wheel for a while this afternoon to give the crew a break after working hard on the cargo and rigging. "They will have to hang a lot of sail while they take lunch in small groups," he said. "I don't know how we can get underway, set sail and all eat at a regular noon meal without staggering the crew. Will you tell Mac and Silas what I am thinking on this?"

"Yes sir, Captain Murphy."

Mac was starting to prepare the Galley for getting the usual big meal for lunch when Andy arrived with the Captains plans for a staggered feeding. "He says we'll have to stagger the crew at the noon meal if we are going to get underway before noon and wanted me to tell you and Silas what he was thinking."

"Go tell Silas to come down to the Galley and tell me how many men will be in each staggered group coming to eat. I need to know how many men will be eating and how much time is allowed before I can plan my workload."

Because Mac sounded somewhat unhappy with the decision to stagger the meals, thus lengthening the feeding time, Andy turned and rushed up on deck to find Silas. He was still on the fo'c'sle watching crews high on the fore and main masts setting the skysails and royals. He gave the message from Mac to Silas and stood watching the men lifting the main yardarm back into its regular place. The main yard was a heavy timber and there were four men on a capstan providing the power to lift it into place.

As Andy stood watching the crew hoisting the yardarm he listened to the squealing of the pulleys as they turned under the pressure of the yardarm's heavy weight. It was not as loud as when they hoisted the boxes of tools onto the barge, it was just more noticeable because they were the only pulleys squealing in protest to the strain they were under. Again Andy was reminded of farm life at home and the many times he had heard pulleys squeal and screech under the tensions of heavy loads. In his mind he could picture a team of oxen pulling a drag loaded with rocks from the garden land where they would no longer be a danger of breaking plowshares.

Once he had seen what everyone was doing to get the Java Sea moving again, he went back to the galley. It was mealtime again and his first duties were to help Mac. Learning about the operation of the ship was secondary.

As he walked in the Galley door, Silas was getting a tongue lashing from Mac about the small size of the groups he was going to send to eat at each sitting. "If I can't have bigger groups of eaters each time I set up the food, Andy and I will be here until midnight trying to feed everyone. I think you can send me eight at a time without shorting yourself of men to get the sails up."

"All you think of is your time. I have to think of my men's time, too. I can't send you all my men and put the sails up alone. You dough-head, I'm the one responsible for getting this ship back out to sea, not you, and I'll send you what I can spare. I still have to get my job done. I will be the nice guy and send you eight at a time. All I ask is, you feed them something they can eat fast and get back up in the rigging."

"I can live with that. Send me the first eight at 12:30. I'll feed them and send them back by 1 pm. Agreed?"

Silas took a moment to answer with a look on his face as if he was deep in thought at the transaction. He replied, "I can live with that. I Agree." He turned and walked out the Galley door, laughing a hearty laugh as he went.

Mac started laughing as soon as Silas was out of hearing range. He gave Andy a cooking pot and told him to go in the storeroom and come back with some fresh carrots to use for carrot sticks at lunch. I am going to make ham and cheese sandwiches. "We have some yellow cake and I can open a jar of strawberries to go with it for dessert. Everybody will like that and it will go fast. They can put the carrot sticks in their pockets and nibble them when they have a chance."

CHAPTER 14

▼

The rigging began to squeak and squeal as the sails filled with air from the light breeze blowing across the harbor at Port of Spain, Trinidad. Andy stood on the poop deck near the wheelman, watching and listening to the sounds of the Java Sea picking up headway, ever so slowly at first, gradually becoming fully borne by the wind. Men were still aloft on the fore and mizzen yardarms making the final adjustments and tightening the sails for the open sea. The ship began to gain a little speed, yet the helmsman held her steady with the bowsprit pointed straight for the land on the northeast entrance to the harbor. Andy began to worry the Java Sea was going to run aground, when the cry went up, "Stand by to come about." Less than a minute later there was another cry, this time, "Hard to starboard, set a course of zero-six-zero."

As the great ship started to come about to starboard the deck began to tilt and Andy had to shift his weight to keep from falling. Clearing the harbor entrance, the breeze began to strengthen, making the sails work harder, keeping the Java Sea moving ever forward. When they reached a point where the land was no longer within sight of the lookout in the crows nest, a new course was set at one-one-zero. With a near following wind, the ship headed in a south by southeasterly direction along the northeast coast of South America.

Captain Murphy was well satisfied with the performance of his crew and called Silas to come up on the poop deck to tell him all men who could be spared would be allowed to spend the afternoon at their leisure. "We will reset the watch at five o'clock after the evening meal. Once you have had your lunch you can relieve me at the helm while I get mine. Tell Mac a sandwich and coffee will be fine, but if he has any more of that cake left, I could enjoy a small piece."

"Yes sir, Captain," Silas replied. "In fact, Mac is supposed to be holding a piece of the cake for me and a couple of others. I feel sure we can come up with a piece for you. In fact, Captain, if you would care to go to lunch first, I will take the helm until you come back."

"No, I will go after you, because I am not very hungry at present. If something happened to delay my return, we would have to call Lt. Brown or one of the helmsmen away from their break time. I think it best you go to lunch ahead of me."

"Yes sir, I shall return as soon as I can."

The rest of the day was uneventful. All hands were enjoying their leisure time. A few were playing cards while others napped in the shade of the large main sail. The Java Sea at first picked up a little speed as the sails were tightened and the yardarms adjusted to pick up more wind. She finally settled at a speed of three and a half to four knots.

Lt. Brown and Andy took a positioning at 5pm and found they were a total of twenty-three knots from their anchorage in the Port of Spain harbor. As usual Andy did the math and Lt. Brown checked his work. The two of them had become a very good navigation team. They liked working together and the Lieutenant thought of Andy as a prime student for the job of understudy navigator. Whenever there was anything unusual in the problem he always consulted and explained things to Andy, enabling him to get a thorough grasp on all aspects of the navigational problem.

Once the navigational job was completed, Andy went to the fo'c'sle and found himself a comfortable seat on a large coil of rope. He laid back and watched the ocean passing under the bowsprit, daydreaming of home and family. He thought about what each might be doing at that particular moment. He was sure Maria and Emily would be in the little one-room schoolhouse on the Annapolis Road. He thought his mother might be in the garden gathering some vegetables for supper. Who else would do it, with him here on the Java Sea?

His father would be coming home from work in about three more hours and he would have to feed the chickens, pigs, milk the cows and bring hay down from the loft to have it handy for morning. After supper he would split wood for the stove or work on any number of farm chores. Andy began to feel a little guilty as he thought about leaving all his farm chores to other family members. He became slightly melancholy as he thought.

That melancholy feeling ended suddenly as he saw a fish come out of water and glide over the wave on wings. It was his first sighting of a flying fish. Just as he was about to think he was seeing things two more came out of water and glided on their wide spread wings. He became excited at what he was seeing and went down on the main deck to find Silas. Before he found Silas, he came upon Ed Smith dozing behind the capstan.

"Ed, you have to come see what I just saw off the bow. There are fish that fly out of the water on big wings. I saw two or three at the same time, all in the air at once. Come see."

"I believe you. All sailors who ply the waters of the Caribbean Sea and tropical Atlantic see flying fish on every trip. They are not really flying, they have big pectoral fins attached right near their gill area which they spread wide and glide on. Sometimes they sail quite a long distance. I was on one ship where two of them flew high enough to land on the main deck."

"Thanks, Ed. I think I will go back and watch them again. They are interesting for a young landlubber like me."

"I'll come with you Andy and we can chat while we watch them. I haven't had much of a chance to get acquainted with you except when we're in the chow hall and you are pretty busy there."

There was a shady spot along the fo'c'sle railing where the mainsail of the foremast was still casting a good shadow. There was a large mooring bitt located in a handy spot where they could sit and talk while watching for flying fish. They made themselves comfortable and Ed started the conversation with a question about Jimmy Mixon.

"Well, Kid, now that you have been filling Jimmy Mixon's shoes for a while what do you think of a sailor's life?"

"I've no complaints. Everyone is good to me and I am getting more familiar with the work each day, so that makes it easier."

"Do you miss the farm life you left behind?"

"Some times when there is no work and once in a while at night, when I can't go to sleep. Most of the time I have enough work and duties to keep me busy. I don't have time to think about the farm often enough that it bothers me."

"What was it like on the farm?

"It was a good life with plenty of work at all times of the year. There was always livestock to care for and feed two or three times a day. I was always busy at home. We had a large farm. There were five of us to do the work. My dad and I did the heavy work and my mother and two sisters did all of the work in the house. They did the cooking, canning, housekeeping, sewing, knitting, laundry and much of the garden weeding. They never ran out of work."

"How old are your sisters?"

"One is about to turn nineteen and the younger one is ten this year. I'd like to get a letter from home to find out how my oldest sister is getting along with Jimmy Mixon. He is working on the farm while I am away and I think they are interested in each other. He might be my brother-in-law when I get back. There's another guy, one Maria went to school with, who might be interested in her as well."

"Which one do you think will win her heart?"

"I really don't know Ed, but my mind tells me Jimmy Mixon would probably be real good to her. He spent so many years on the Java Sea, after he was twelve-years-old, I would think he'd be real good to a wife and family," Andy said.

"Ralph Gleason is the other man in the picture with Jimmy and Maria. Ralph owns a small shipyard down river from the farm near Annapolis. He and Maria were in school together at our one room schoolhouse. Ralph was three grades ahead of Maria. In a small school all kids know each other and when Maria needed a box to carry her teaching books, I got Ralph to build it for her. He gave her the box. We assembled and painted it at home. Ralph and Maria made a date to go to dinner at a fancy restaurant near Annapolis. I left on the Java Sea before they dated. Ralph might make a good husband to Maria because they grew up in the same area and have plenty of mutual friends. At least they know something about each other from school."

"Well, kid, I'll tell you something. There's no telling which one of the men will be best for Maria. The final choice is going to be hers. You better go along with whatever she decides or you'll have your sister angry at you, which could upset you and perhaps some others from your family."

"Yeah Ed, I know it's going to be her decision. I just want the best for my sister because she has always been very good to me. Being the oldest of the three of us, she was the leader and gave Emily and me good advice on things we asked her about. She's like my Mom and Dad with a good sound brain in her head. She makes good decisions. I think I can count on her making the right decision between Ralph and Jimmy for a husband."

"I'd offer her my hand if I wasn't so much older and nearly worn out from all the years at sea," Ed remarked, with a good sound chuckle adding emphasis.

"You don't look old and worn out to me. I think you'd make a good husband and father for a wife and children."

"I try to be, kid. My wife doesn't think I am a good husband and I have been at sea for so long my kids don't even know me."

"You mean you're married and have children?" Andy asked.

"I have a wife in Halifax with thirteen year old twin boys and a girl eight. I haven't seen them in over two years. One of the boys wrote me a letter over a year ago. Jimmy Mixon read it to me. I got another in Baltimore a few days before we left on this trip. They're not a family a man can be proud of and I'm not a man they can be proud of so it levels out."

"That's too bad Ed. A man and his family should be close in their relationship with each other. There's got to be a warm feeling among them. My Dad says a family that prays together, stays together. He thinks being close to one's God is most important in family relations. I think he is right. My Christian upbringing is what keeps me close to my family. I think it is what keeps them close to me. We are a loving family. I'll pray you and your family can get closer together in your relationship," Andy told him.

"Say, you're a smart kid and I appreciate what you just told me. I hope your prayers work because I would like to be closer to my family. If I could go home after a voyage and find them waiting for me and I could put my arms around them and give them a hug, it would be perfect. I get melancholy about my family, but not knowing how to write, I can't tell them how I feel. I never had any school where I lived and we were always busy trying to get enough to eat. Ma made all our clothes. I got my first store bought clothes when I went to sea."

Andy felt sorry for Ed Smith when he heard him pouring out his tale of hardship. He thought about it, wondering what if it had been me telling the story. I'd like someone to help me improve my lot in life and not have to continue struggling on in ignorance. The more thought he put into the subject the more he realized he might be able to help Ed after work at night or between watches if Silas would allow the time. He decided he would check with Silas and Mac to see what could be done.

Ed got up from his seat on the bitt and said, "I have to go on watch at the helm as soon as the evening meal is over. I have the early watch this evening. I think I will go get ready and we can have another chat one of these fine days. I enjoyed talking with you this afternoon Andy. You impress me as a smart young man. I wish I had some education like you do. See you later, kid."

"I enjoyed chatting with you and will look forward to another time when we have a chance to do it again," Andy told him.

Mac was a good cook and often prepared meals requiring little clean up time, especially evening meals when he and Andy were tired from their long day of work, much of it spent in the hot galley. Tonight's supper was one of the quick cleanup meals and they were freed from the galley and chow hall before six o'clock.

With the sun still above the horizon, Andy went looking for Lt. Brown to find out what time he planned to take the position readings. He found him asleep in a hammock he had hung between the two stanchions in his room, gently rocking back and forth with the rolls of the ship. Andy watched for a minute trying to decide whether to wake him. He decided to let him sleep.

Picking up the sextant, a pencil and paper, he headed up to the main deck to take the position readings himself. He had done it before and would have a surprise for Lt. Brown when he awakened. From the poop deck, he got good readings on the late day sun. He figured the ship's position on the paper and decided they were at 8 degrees North and 46 degrees west.

After checking the figures he went back to Lt. Brown's cabin and found the Lieutenant was awake, sitting in a chair with a sleepy look, while putting on his shoes. The Lieutenant said, "Hello, Andy. I was just going to look for you. We need to take the position before the sun gets any lower to the horizon."

"I came in before and didn't want to wake you, so I went up and took the position myself. Here is my work sheet. It is a good chance to check my work if you take another position now. There's about a half hour time lapse."

"Good thinking, Andy. As soon as I get my eyes fully open I'll do it again and see what kind of position I come up with. If you're not busy, stick around."

With the Lieutenant carrying the sextant, Andy carrying the paper and pencil, the two went back to the main deck for the Lieutenant's turn at taking readings. It was noticeable to Andy the sun had gone lower since his readings but was still high enough above the horizon for good position angles. He believed he had made correct readings and math. He hoped Mr. Brown's work would prove him right.

The Lt. sat down on the edge of one of the lifeboat davits to do the math on his readings. When he was finished he had the same answer as Andy with the exception of decimal remainders. Taking the difference of mathematical leftovers into consideration meant the ship had moved from when Andy took his readings. Lt. Brown decided the two of them had the same answer, the difference being the small amount of ship movement between readings.

"I find nothing wrong with your work, lad. You did a good job. Let's go down and plot the chart positions for today and I'll let the Captain know you can do the navigational problem all alone. He'll be pleased to know about that."

CHAPTER 15

▼

The following morning, as Andy walked into the chow hall, he noticed Silas was sitting alone in the seat near the galley door. He walked over to him and asked if there would be a time today when they could sit down and discuss something Andy had on his mind.

"I have a large hawser to splice and will be working all morning in the bo's'n locker. If you come down there after you get your chores finished with Mac and Captain Murphy, you can have my ear at least until it is time to get lunch. How does that sound?"

"That's great. I don't think it will take long. I want your advice on something and will see you when I am clear of my usual duties. Thanks, Silas," Andy said.

Andy stepped into the galley and exchanged Good Mornings with Mac. He could see the coffee was hot so he prepared a tray for the Captain and Lieutenant. "I'll be back as soon as I deliver this coffee," he told Mac, then asked, "What's for breakfast?"

"We're having creamed beef on toasted biscuits with sugar dipped donuts and coffee. I also have a few oranges left and there may be enough for everyone to have one. I'll try to pick up more, if a vendor comes along side, when we are in Recife or Salvador, Brazil. They have decent fruit and vegetables at those ports. If this nice breeze holds, we should be in and out of there by the end of this month.

The sun was just peeking above the horizon as Andy walked aft with the morning coffee for the officers. It was still dark enough on the main deck he had to watch his footing not to trip. Coiled ends that were hung nice and neat at sunset have a way of working themselves loose and dropping to where they will be underfoot in the early morning. Picking up and recoiling those loose ends is one of the first daily jobs on a sailing vessel.

Captain Murphy was up and in his lavatory shaving when Andy entered. He sat the coffee on the desk and said, loud enough for him to hear, "Here's your coffee Captain Murphy, Sir."

"Thank you, Andy. Did Mac say what he is having for breakfast?"

"Creamed beef on toasted biscuits. Sugar dipped donuts and coffee. He has some oranges and thinks there is enough so everyone can have one," Andy replied.

Lt. Brown spoke up and said, "I'll take the coffee and donuts. He can give my orange and the creamed beef to some hungry deckhand," adding, with a shivering motion to his body, "Brrr, I don't like creamed beef nor oranges."

Captain Murphy told him, "By the time you get back to civilization you may like creamed beef as much as you like apple pie, and everyone likes apple pie." He added a little chuckle to let Andy and the Lieutenant know he was joking about it.

"We'll eat in the chow hall after the crew is finished. Because we are under sail and should stay on this course for a few days at least. It will help lighten the load for you and Mac," the captain told Andy as Lt. Brown nodded agreement.

"Today will be a good day for you to take the position sightings again. We should get in some good practice, while we are under full sail, and in an area where nothing unusual happens this time of year," Lt. Brown said.

"What time should I report to you?" Andy asked.

"If 9:30 will work out for you, why don't we plan on it?"

"Good, Lieutenant Brown, Sir, I'll be there."

When Andy had completed his work in the chow hall and galley he headed to the bo's'n locker to talk to Silas. He walked in and stood beside him as he was working on the hawser splice. He didn't notice Willie Wispor sitting on the deck in the far corner of the locker sewing on a large sail. He said, "Good Morning again, Silas. I am here to talk to you about something and get your opinion about it."

"Good Morning, Andy. Why don't you go right ahead and start right in, I'll wait until you finish before I answer or ask questions?"

"That sounds good to me," Andy replied.

"While we were on our leisure time yesterday afternoon I went up on the bow and was watching the flying fish with Ed Smith. We had a good chat and I learned he has a wife and children in Halifax, Nova Scotia, Canada. He also can't read and write. He said someone reads his mail to him.

"I have given it a lot of thought since yesterday and think I can help him. I can teach him to read and write. We'll be on this voyage for about two years or more depending on available freight at our ports of call. I'd like to set aside some of my off duty time to helping him.

"If you had been with us yesterday and heard him explaining about not getting letters from home you would approve of my trying to teach him to read and write.

"One of his sons wrote him a letter and it is difficult for them at home not being able to hear from him. I feel sorry for him and his family and would like to help, so they can all benefit from it. Do you think my teaching him will be alright?"

"I see no reason anyone should object, unless of course, Ed Smith thinks you are singling him out to let others know he has a problem. There are others in the crew who are in the same boat when it comes to reading and writing."

"I could help them, too."

"I think it best you talk to Captain Murphy about it before anyone else is approached. As for the idea of helping those who would like to learn reading and writing, I am all for it, as long as it doesn't interfere with the ship's work and watches. In fact, if you would like me to do it, I'll set up a meeting with Lt. Brown and Captain Murphy where we can present your proposal and see if they will agree it is a sound thing to do."

"That's a good idea. I'll wait until I hear from you before I mention it to Ed Smith. I appreciate your help and support on this, Silas. It is nearing time to take the positioning. I better run so I don't keep Lt. Brown waiting for his helper."

"How do you like working with Lt. Brown, and do you like taking positions twice a day?"

"I think Lt. Brown is a nice man. He's a lot like you in many ways. He's always ready to help me and teach me things about navigation, where you teach me things about seamanship and the everyday operation of the ship. I have good teachers as I learn the ways of the sea. Everyone treats me well and they're always adding to my understanding of how the overall ship handling comes together. Everyone has to do their best job, even me, the cabin boy."

"Glad to have you as a member of the crew, Andy. I'll see you later."

As Andy turned to leave he saw Willie sewing the sail and sitting in the far corner of the bo's'n locker. He wondered how much he had heard of his conversation with Silas. He knew Willie was one to run with stories and rumors all over the ship. There was nothing he could do about it now and with Lt. Brown waiting for him, he put it out of his mind and hurried down to the navigation table. The Lieutenant was waiting with a couple of charts spread before him.

"I was delayed a little while talking to Silas about an idea I have to help some of the crew members. I hope I didn't keep you waiting long," he told Lt. Brown.

"No, Andy. I just finished getting all the things we will need placed in this new box the carpenter made for the navigational equipment. We can use this new box to carry the sextant and other equipment, use the top of it as a desk while on deck and even sit on it as we figure out new positions. I think it will be a godsend to have all our things in one sturdy box. It was nice of William Isley to make it for us when he didn't have an order to do it."

"It's a good looking box and not too big for one man to carry. He sure finished it nice with the brown stain and spar varnish," Andy remarked.

"Actually, this box is not stained. Carpenter William Isley told me the brown color is the natural color of the wood. He used only varnish to cover it. He said it is an Argentine wood named quebracho and will turn a darker brown with time. So, we can watch our box change from the medium brown it is today to a deep, dark brown as we use it in our navigational duties. What do you think of that?" The Lt. asked.

"I guess it will be quite interesting, seeing it change color while sealed with spar varnish," Andy answered.

They went up to the main deck and as usual Andy took the first readings and did the math to find the ship's position. When he had completed the math, Lt. Brown did his set of readings and came up with a different position.

"We can't be 28 miles different in position. Something is wrong," Lt Brown said. "Here, you check my figures and I'll check yours to see if we find any mistakes.

After going over the figures both agreed the answers were right to the two sets of figures. Andy asked to look at both sets of figures at the same time. When he took the paper they had each used for their math, Andy immediately picked up on the fact both papers started with a different initial reading. He called it to Lt. Brown's attention, whereupon he began laughing.

"That's a good eye you have there, Andy, you made a good catch on the different figures. Actually it was a test I pulled on you to find out if you would catch the error. You did a good job of it. When I took the sextant from you I gave the angle setting a very small adjustment so the reading would be a slightly larger number. I'm glad you caught the error. It shows you are paying attention to the details of navigation. Congratulations on your superior work."

"Thank you Mr. Brown. Shall we do the position again to check it."

"That won't be necessary. Your figures are right. We can let it go now until the afternoon reading."

"I also figured out how many miles we covered since our last position check. We have covered 88.6 knots since yesterday afternoon. When it is converted to miles, we have traveled 82 miles. Is that good?"

"Yes, when the lack of a strong wind is taken into consideration. Captain Murphy will make an average of 240 miles a day on a trip like this. Right now he doesn't have enough wind. In about 3 to 5 days we will be having more favorable winds for the Java Sea as we head more southerly along the coast of South America."

As Andy walked back to the galley, Silas called to him from the fo'c'sle deck and told him he wanted to talk to him. Silas and four of the crewmen were coiling the big hawser into a box at the corner of the fo'c'sle deck where it would be stored until needed. Rumor had it the Java Sea would not be tying up anywhere until they reached Recife, Brazil. The ship chandler there already had his orders to replenish their needs. Because there would be a good load of supplies coming aboard they expected to stay at the dock for three to four days. Mac was grumbling about starving to death if the Java Sea didn't get a wind to move her faster.

With Andy standing beside him on the fo'c'sle deck, Silas said, "I have an appointment with Captain Murphy to talk about your idea of education for the crew. We'll go see him at 2:30 this afternoon. Mac knows about it. He would like you back to help him at no later than 4 o'clock. I think we can do it, don't you?"

"Golly, we should be back to the galley in a half hour if we start at 2:30. If you and the Captain don't spend a lot of time talking, it shouldn't take long at all. Do you need me for anything else right now?"

"No."

"I'll go work with Mac. He should be starting lunch about now."

"Are you still practicing your swing up into the rigging?"

"Yes, watch." Andy grabbed the foremast shroud and made an easy swing up around it to land on the first ratline in a crouched position exactly as Silas had shown him when the training began two weeks ago.

"That's a good job. Tomorrow we'll start climbing. By the time I am finished with you, I'll have you going up one side of the mast and coming down the other head first." Silas ended with a good chuckle at his remark and thinking of Andy climbing down head first.

Andy came right back at him with, "Just as long as you don't require me to grow a tail to climb with, I'll do my best."

At that point one of the men helping Silas coil the hawser rolled out a big thunderous laugh and said to Silas, "Hey, boss, the kid is sharp. He got back at you good that time."

Arriving in the chow hall, Andy found Mac carrying a big stack of plates to the table for the next meal. After washing his hands and putting on an apron, Andy said, "I'm sorry I am a little late, I'll take over now and get the chow hall set up for lunch."

"Are you getting so many irons in the fire you can't keep up with your normal duties? If you are we can make other arrangements on some of this mealtime work," Mac said to him.

Andy wasn't sure if Mac was a little angry because he was a few minutes late, or trying to impress him with a dose of authority. He decided the best answer would be no answer. What could he say, Mac was right, he was late to work and that's it, period. He kept quiet and kept working.

CHAPTER 16

▼

For the next five days nothing much happened. Everyone was busy with the regular routine of keeping the Java Sea on course and sailing at her best. Two days ago the lookout in the crows nest called out 'Sail Ho.' He had seen it from his perch high above the deck, but it was never seen by those on deck. Silas kept Andy's climbing schedule moving along. During one rain squall, he was allowed to climb half way to the platform where the lower mast and the upper mast joined. Andy followed instructions and climbed slow and carefully as he got the feeling of the ratlines under his feet and in his hands. He practiced every chance he could get time away from other duties. After a week of climbing he was allowed to go to the point where the main and topmast joined. His next step would be to climb past the joining platform and head on up the topmast. Silas had a good talk with him and instilled him with the need for safety in high climbing.

After watching Andy practice his climbing routine, everyone agreed he was doing a good job and learning the right way for a beginner to climb. Silas told him, "If you keep climbing the same way you are climbing as a learner, you'll be good at it in a few months. Just never get smart-alecky or take chances. Always think of yourself and safety as the first requirements."

"I think I can handle climbing better as my time at it increases and I have more experience. I will admit it is a strange feeling to be aloft with the ship pitching and rolling so far below you. Those sudden jerks at the end of a roll or pitch have a way of letting you know you could be tossed overboard, or to the deck, if you don't hang on tightly. It's also exciting."

"You sound like you have a good understanding of climbing. You must always remember it is one hand for you and one hand for the ship. Don't ever let go with both hands at the same time or you might be tossed off the mast. Always make sure your feet are firmly planted on the ratlines or footropes. You have to protect yourself. I cannot express that enough as you become a climber. Of course, your main goal is to become an officer and eventually a Captain in command of your own ship."

"Thank you Silas for all the attention and care you put into my training on the Java Sea. You're a good teacher for me. I must get on with some of my duties in the officer's quarters. If you don't need me longer, I'll go down to the Captain's cabin, remake the bed and pick the room up before lunchtime."

"You go right ahead Andy there'll be plenty of time to talk climbing before we get to Baltimore again."

With that thought in mind Cabin Boy Andy Murphy headed for the Officers Quarters to do daily routine cleaning. Entering the door with happy thoughts in his head he was taken aback as he saw the room was in shambles with papers, charts, maps, books and a myriad of other stuff scattered all over the rooms. One of the officers had left the stern windows and a couple of starboard side portholes open allowing the wind to come through the cabin in full force. Closing the portholes first, he went to work picking up all the maps and charts, sorting them into two piles on the chart table. He followed this effort by gathering other miscellaneous papers and made a single pile of them on the captain's desk. Next came several odds and ends like clothing, bedding, towels and napkins. Lt. Brown's coffee cup had been knocked over and spilled about a half cup of coffee over his desk and into his chair. As he was cleaning up that part of the mess, Lt. Brown walked in and after looking around asked, "What happened in here?"

"When I came in a little more than a half hour ago, I found the stern windows and starboard side portholes open. There was a strong wind coming in through the stern and blowing things around. I closed the portholes and have been picking things up," Andy replied.

"How did you ever sort it out without one of us here to guide you?" the Lieutenant wanted to know.

"I put maps and charts in two different piles on the chart table. All the other papers and books are on the Captain's desk. I just finished cleaning up your desk and chair where the coffee cup was upset. I'll make the beds and straighten up your closets before I leave. You and the captain will have to go through these piles to sort out where things belong. I wouldn't know where to begin," Andy informed the Lieutenant.

"The captain won't be happy about this mess. Perhaps you could help me for a while and we can sort out what are my navigational papers and his ship's records."

"I'm sorry, sir, I have to go to the galley to help Mac get the noon meal ready. I am already running late. I will probably be finished about two o'clock. I could help you after that if you like."

"That's all right, you do your regular duty and I will work on this to see how much I can accomplish. When you have time come back and help me finish the job. We'll let it go at that for now."

Walking to the galley, Andy ran through his mind the attitude and actions of Lt. Brown over the mess in Officers Quarters. He thought the Lt. was extremely nervous over the problem. Perhaps the Lt. was the one who left the windows and portholes open where the wind could do the damage. Lt. Brown acted like he expected Captain Murphy to be very angry with him. The Captain had always been very careful when airing the Quarters out not to do it when there was a strong breeze coming in the back windows. On the basis of his thoughts he decided it was Lt. Brown's mistake which caused the problem. He decided to forget it for there were many more important things he needed to remember.

After being released by Mac, Andy went to help the Lieutenant. He had sorted all the papers out and told Andy he wouldn't be needed. He headed for the fo'c'sle to find out what he could learn from the deck crew. On his way forward Willie Wispor, who was standing a lookout watch, saw him and hollered down from the crows nest to ask if he had seen the whales off the port bow. Andy replied, "Not today. I saw some when we first left Chesapeake Bay."

"There's a big pod of them heading north for the summer. They look like humpbacks that are behind schedule. They should be farther north at this time of year. You should take a look off the bow."

"Thanks Willie. I'll take a look before I go find Silas."

"He's in the carpenter shop with William Isley. They're designing a new table to fit the corner of the chow hall so there will be additional light to play cards and checkers on free time, Willie told him.

The whales were putting on a show with their tails slapping the water and giant heads rising into the air as high as a two story building. Andy enjoyed the show for five minutes before going to the carpenter shop to check with Silas on his afternoon schedule. He was not the type of boy to take advantage of his position and hide from work, but rather, went looking for his next duty. It was a trait that all of the crew admired in their new cabin boy. They didn't have to browbeat him to get him to work. He was punctual. He was industrious. Once shown how to do a job he never had to be shown again. He got it the first time.

Silas gave him the time off so he went back to the Fo'c'sle and watched the whales until they were too far away to enjoy. Because of the distance, they didn't look any larger than the small flying fish he had seen several days ago. He decided to go back and watch the helmsman steer the ship, check on her course, speed, read the log and find out if the helmsman would like a cup of coffee brought up to him. He climbed the six steps to the poop deck and went in the wheelhouse. He was not surprised to find Rosco Quinn on the wheel. Rosco stood more afternoon wheel watches than any other man aboard the Java Sea. "Hi Rosco," he said. "Would you like me to get you a cup of coffee?"

"That sounds good to me. I'd like it with two teaspoons of sugar but none of that imitation creamer."

"I'll be right back."

When Andy returned with the coffee, Silas was sitting on the wheel box talking to Rosco. He asked, "Is that my coffee?"

"This is for Rosco. I will go get you a cup if you want."

"I have to talk to Mac and will have a cup with him while we go over business."

Looking over the log, Andy discovered the ship was on a new heading five degrees more to the south. The log was still indicating a good speed with a strong, steady wind aft of the starboard beam. Everything was going well for the ship and she was making good time toward her next port of call. It would not be long before she crossed the Equator and came to a heading even closer to due south. The ocean water was not as salty as it had been and when he inquired about it from Lt. Brown, the Lt. explained they were near the mouth of the great Amazon River. The Amazon empties so much fresh water into the sea it freshens the water for miles out from the land. Some ships have been known to dip cooking water when they are off the Amazon far enough they can no longer see land from their crows nest. "It's an amazing phenomenon to have a river with its fresh water overpower the ocean. No other river in the world can do it as far out to sea as the Amazon. There have been claims of fresh water over two hundred miles off shore. If it is true, it is almost unbelievable."

Silas got up from the wheel box and called Andy to go with him to talk to Mac. "I want to see what kind of a schedule I can work out, for you with Mac, if Captain Murphy approves you teaching others to read and write. I'll have to set the watches to coincide with teaching time, because I want those needing the lessons off duty at the time you will be holding a class. Your schedule with Mac may have to be adjusted to get you in class when I can get the men there. Once it is worked out with Mac, we can talk to the Captain and get his approval."

"I didn't intend to hold regular classes. I thought I could work with one man at a time," Andy informed him.

"My idea is to have classes so the men can work together in their spare time learning from each other. They'd be able to help one another learn faster, with an interest in each other's progress."

"That sounds logical, too. I'd be willing to do it your way and if we find it isn't working we can always shift to my way."

"Well, we may find the Captain has a different way or doesn't want to use the time to educate people about something they should have learned as youngsters. I think we'll have to wait to see what he says."

Andy remained silent for a couple of minutes as he thought it over. He then said, "I think I got it figured out. It should work if I divide the class into those who can attend on different days using odd and even numbered days as a guide or Monday and Tuesday for one group and Thursday and Friday for the second group. What do you think of that idea?"

"I think it sounds like you expect to see most of the crew in your classroom. There may not be that many interested, including Ed Smith who you want to help. The more we talk about it the more I realize we need to work it out with Mac, know your free time, set a schedule and talk with Captain Murphy. After that we still need to know how many crew members will be interested in learning to read and write."

After they talked it over with Mac, it took two days to work out a schedule for Andy to hold classes. They did not mention it to the crew for fear of rumors and possible disappointments if things failed to materialize as planned. The following day they held their meeting with Captain Murphy. Lt. Brown came in part way through the meeting and was told what had transpired before he arrived. The discussion lasted three-fourths of an hour and the Captain and Lieutenant indicated they thought it was a good idea with an exception; Andy doesn't get worn out or overworked.

Silas and Andy went to the bo's'n locker and discussed what they would do to start the program for the crew. They decided to talk to individual members on a one on one basis as the best idea, followed with scheduling individuals to a class meeting. After a few days of talking to the crew, they found there were only three members interested in the schooling. Ed Smith and Doug Stewart signed up at the first chance they were given. Ship's carpenter William Isley was a little hesitant and was nearly left off the list because of it. He turned into an asset for the schooling because of his skill with tools. He made a large blackboard and a small lap-desk for each student. The officers provided pencils and a bag full of paper that was good on one side to do lessons. Class started on the same day the Java Sea made a course correction to another more southerly heading which would bring her to Recife, Brazil for her third port of call.

Andy gave a short introduction about what they would learn. He agreed to go with each individual to the ship's library to pick out an easy book to read for their first attempt. He told them the most important thing to learn as a starter was the alphabet.

"You must know the alphabet to read and write," he told them, introducing them to the alphabet song he had learned at school when he was in his first year. Shy about singing the alphabet at first they gradually relaxed and sang along with Andy leading them. The second night as they were singing the alphabet, Silas and Lieutenant Brown walked through the area trying not to look intrusive to the class. They botched the attempt. After class, Silas cornered Andy in the chow hall and said, "The Lieutenant told me, 'If the frogs in a pond could sing the alphabet in English, they'd sound just like your school choir'." Following that, Silas leaned over the table and proceeded to laugh and snort at his own joke.

Andy looked at him teasingly and said, "Oink, Oink," turned on his heel and walked out.

CHAPTER 17

▼

The weather had been very hot and seemed to be getting hotter. Andy started sleeping on deck behind the wheelhouse to be more comfortable in the cooler night air. The helmsman with the wheel watch at 4am would wake him to start his day. He went to his sea bag and got a towel to dry off then hoisted two buckets of sea water up where he could pour it over himself as an impromptu shower. He thought he noticed the water was not as salty as it had been. He believed he must be dreaming. The ocean is the ocean, the water is the same all over and should be just as salty here as it is in Baltimore or Trinidad or anywhere. Still, it did seem diluted with fresh water. It felt somewhat better on his skin. Then he remembered what Lt. Brown had told him about the Amazon and a few other big rivers. He decided the Java Sea must be nearing the mouth of the Amazon.

Later that morning, when he and Lt. Brown were taking the ship's position he told the Lt. "I have discovered the water is not as salty now. What I learned from you about rivers is coming true where we are now sailing."

"Yes, we are getting much closer to the Amazon and should have all fresh water around us tomorrow and the next day. The wildlife you see will be different also. In fact, it is not impossible to see a crocodile if we get in close enough, although I expect Captain Murphy to stay off shore a little more than most Captains do. Captain Murphy is a real deep water man when he is sailing between ports."

"How is your teaching going with the older men," the Lieutenant asked?

"We've only had a few days in the class. I think it is going well. I have not received any complaints. The men are eager to learn. They act as if it is a privilege to have me teaching them to read and write. They have the alphabet song memorized and are coming along well in the recognition of individual characters. I am teaching them both capital and lower case letters at the same time. I made three drawings of the alphabet with capital and lowercase letters so each man could have his own. They are possessive and protective of them. I'm convinced they are interested in learning, which is good."

"You seem to be as interested as they are and should be commended for helping them. I doubt there are many cabin boys your age willing to teach a group of older sailors the fundamentals of reading and writing while working a voyage. I tip my hat to you Andy," Lt. Brown commented.

That afternoon Andy went into the galley to find Mac. He was feeling terrible and was shaking with the chills. He told Mac, "I think I am sick. I have the chills and feel like I am freezing. It started yesterday. It's getting worse today. Do we have any medicine for it?"

"Come here and let me feel your forehead." With a hand on Andy's forehead he said, "It feels real hot to me. We better check with John Simmons our acting ship's doctor. He knows more about these things. He studied some medicine at Yale in Connecticut a few years ago."

Silas walked in and asked "Can I get some coffee this time of day?"

"Better than that, you can get John Simmons down here for the kid. He seems to have a fever. Feel his forehead."

"He's got a fever for sure. He feels real hot to my hand," Silas replied.

Silas sent Willie Wispor up to the crows nest to relieve John Simmons long enough for him to come down and attend to Andy's needs. As soon as John checked him over he said, "This boy must lie down and be cooled off with sea water brought up from fifty or more feet down. If he develops any pain, I have some pain medicine. I can give him small amounts a couple of times a day. Keeping him as cool as possible with no activity is the best we can do until the fever breaks. I'll go get the pills while the rest of you carry him up on the main deck where he can have some shade and be cooled with water. It is good we're off the mouth of the Amazon where the water will be quite fresh."

Everyone that could be spared from ship's work was put to work making a comfortable spot for Andy behind the wheelhouse. An improvised bunk with a hammock stretched between the head and foot became his new bed. One of the smaller jib sails was hung from the roof of the wheelhouse to shelter him from the sun and tropical squalls. Andy protested all the attention, while at the same time going along with it, knowing full well he had never felt this sick before.

Water was brought up from the depths and poured slowly, a ladle at a time, over Andy as he lay on the net hammock. Every man on the Java Sea tended to his needs at one time or another including both of the officers and Silas. For three days he ate nothing, depending only on water for subsistence. John Simmons gave him one fourth of a white pill, refusing to tell what medicine was in the pill. About 9:15 on the third morning the call came down from the crows nest, "Sail Ho, two points on the starboard bow and closing." Those on the raised poop and forecastle decks looked ahead to see if they could tell what was coming toward them. It appeared to be a brigantine with square rigged fore and main masts, and a schooner rigged after mast. This was quite a common way to rig a ship for deep water fishing. The after boom could be rigged over the side where small boats could tie up while they were at the fishing grounds.

As the new ship drew closer, it appeared they were trying to intersect the Java Sea's course. Captain Murphy came on deck and decided it was a whaler. If he was heading north, he had probably been to the South Pacific hunting whales and was on his way back to the United States. New England is noted for its many schooner and brigantine fishing vessels. He reckoned it would be another hour before the two ships closed to hailing distance. There was not enough wind to make much more than a knot or two in speed since coming into the fresh water area of the Amazon.

Once they reached hailing distance, the two captains introduced themselves and their home ports. The brigantine was the Marie Luce out of New Bedford, Massachusetts. Her captain was Alex Fleming a Nova Scotia man. He asked if the Java Sea had any mail to be posted in the States or any messages for the home office in Baltimore. There were some personal letters and Captain Murphy had a few shipping bills-of-laden he requested to be delivered to the home office. In return for the convenience of the favor, a few supplies were taken from the Java Sea for the Marie Luce and her crew. Captain Murphy had a small boat lowered to make the delivery across the short distance between them.

When Captain Fleming was informed the Java Sea cabin boy was sick with what appeared to be a tropical fever he asked, "What are you doing to break the fever?"

He was told, cold water wash downs and a liquid diet of water, plus a little broth. The kid is really sick and has no interest in food, or the broth as a matter of fact.

"Don't leave yet. I have something in my cabin that will help him." Captain Fleming went to his cabin and came back with a piece of tree limb. He told Silas. "Scrape the wood into the finest shavings you can make, boil a cup of shavings for fifteen minutes in a pint of water. Drain the water and juice through a piece of good, clean cloth. Give the boy a teaspoon of liquid every five or six hours. It will take his fever down."

"What is it?" Silas asked.

"I expected you to ask that question. Now, I must tell you, I don't know. I had it given to me by a native medicine man from a small Argentine village. I only know it works. The natives call the tree quebracho. Please trust me, for the lad's sake."

"I think anything is worth a try at this point. I certainly will talk to our Captain, and convince him to use it," Silas said.

"It has been a pleasure meeting you Java Sea sailors and I hope our courses cross again. I know you must leave because you will have a long row back as it is, Captain Fleming said.

"We're indebted to you for this tree limb you say will cure our cabin boy. I wish you smooth sailing and a brisk following wind on your journey home." The two men shook hands and Captain Fleming made it a point to shake the hands of the rowers as well. Departing the Marie Luce, they noticed there were at least two miles to row to the Java Sea before suppertime.

As soon as the small boat reached the side of the Java Sea, it was taken into tow with a short line holding its bow, while another line was placed to keep the stern in close to the side of the ship. The rowers broke into a cheer, acting happy to be relieved from their long, tiring row. A small climbing ladder was lowered for the boat crew to board the ship. Silas carried the piece of tree limb provided by Captain Fleming and called for William Isley and John Simmons to follow him. With the two men following, he went down to Captain Murphy's office and knocked on the door. The Captain opened the door and asked, "What can I do for you, Silas?"

"Captain Murphy, I would like to talk to you about some medicine, given to us by Captain Fleming. He says it will cure Andy's fever. I'd like to discuss it with you and answer your questions. I have Simmons and Isley with me because they may know something about what I have here," Silas said, as he lifted the tree limb for Captain Murphy to see.

"What is this and how is it used?"

"Captain Fleming told us it is a piece of quebracho tree limb. It was given to him by an old native medicine man in Argentina. He instructed us to scrape fine shavings from it, boil them and feed Andy the juice as medicine every five hours. He impressed me as a sincere man with concern for Andy. As for the limb and his other claims, I only know the facts I have given you."

After passing the piece of limb around for all to examine, Bill Isley spoke up and said, "I'll vouch for the fact the wood is quebracho. There is no other wood like it in weight, texture and color I am aware of in this part of the world. Beyond that I wouldn't have any additional knowledge of quebracho."

"I may have something I can add to the discussion," John Simmons, said. "While I was acquainted with the medical students at Yale, they often talked about the unknown number of new medicines to be found in jungles all over the world. I remember the odd name quebracho being a pain and fever reducer, just beginning to be noticed by researchers. Jungle natives use it to induce relaxation and cure pain. I don't have any details, only a general knowledge from student chatter about the wonders to be found in jungle plants."

"Based on what we know at this point, Andy's extremely high fever and our wishes to see him well again, is reason we are obliged to try this as a medicine for him. If we all agree, I will allow it with the understanding we cease the treatment if we suspect the slightest unfavorable reaction in Andy which might be caused by this treatment," Captain Murphy stated to the other three. They were all in agreement with his decision.

When the three crewmen were back on the main deck again, they sang praises of their skipper and were pleased they may have some help for Andy right in their hands, in the form of a muddy brown colored tree limb. Silas said, "Bill, you take the limb down to the carpenter shop and scrape some clean, fine shavings for our first batch of Andy Juice. I'll take John with me. We will go convince Mac we have the Captain's permission to give Andy the juice we're going to make."

As Silas entered the galley door, followed a step behind by John, Mac started yelling, "Get out, Get out," causing Silas to speedily step back, nearly knocking John to the deck.

"Hey, you old goat, you nearly killed our doctor. You better not yell at us like that or we won't have anyone left who can cure Andy," Silas yelled back at him.

"No coffee for you," came back at them.

"We're not here for coffee. We want you to boil some shavings for us as soon as Bill Isley brings them down. He should be here in a couple of minutes. In the meantime we will explain what we are going to try on Andy to lower his fever more than the cold water is doing."

"If you just said you want me to boil shavings, forget it. My pots and pans are for cooking. I don't boil shavings in them. Shavings, you're nuts. Is the tropical heat getting too much for our ship's boatswains mate. I hope so, you faker."

"Talk to John here, he'll tell you about the new medicine we got from the whale ship we think it will help Andy. Captain Murphy already approved it."

"That's right," John said.

Mac cooled down and offered to serve them a cup of coffee, which both men rejected knowing full well Mac was extremely tired from working long hours since being deprived of Andy's help. They went on to explain about the procedure for making the concoction they nicknamed Andy's Juice. His reply was he had heard of the quebraco tree and knew it stained whatever it was cooked in. He wanted to know what they intended to use as a cooking pot. When they said they thought he would use some of the ship's cookware, he got excited again and only quieted when Silas and John agreed to buy him a replacement kettle as soon as they docked in Recife.

Bill Isley came with a small box of fine shavings held out in front of him as he walked down the steps. Silas got up from his seat at a table and took the box. He and Mac went into the galley where Mac prepared a small pan to boil the cup of shavings. Within fifteen minutes he had the water boiling and the wood shavings began producing a milky color to the water. Soon it turned to a yellow tint and didn't change color again. Silas took a teaspoon from the drawer and tasted a very small sample of the liquid. Immediately his face screwed into a contortion that anyone could see meant sour, bitter. When he got his composure back, he said, "That is the most sour-bitter taste I have ever, in my lifetime, tasted."

"So now all you have to do is get the kid to take it," Mac said. "I think you're just the man for the job, feeding a lamebrain concoction to a young cabin boy who is helplessly sick in bed."

"Yeah, Mac, you might be right. But I'll tell you one thing, I'll do it if it will help the kid and all we know at this point is, it will."

CHAPTER 18

▼

The log book of the Java Sea had an entry for August 17, 1807 reporting the first dose of the new medicine was given to Andy at 7pm. The day of the week was not mentioned. A detailed description of who was involved and the expected result was noted. Silas and John Simmons administered the dose according to directions they had received from Captain Fleming. They thought Andy was in somewhat of a stupor as he continually mumbled something about pirates aboard the Java Sea. He was in and out of a semi-conscious state as they worked over him. He took the medicine without complaint. He was given a cold water wash down and settled into a deeper stupor. He rested comfortably until a short time before the midnight watch changed.

At the watch change, Ed Smith and Willie Wispor administered the second dose of the new found medicine. Andy believed them to be pirates and called Willie 'Captain Jack' before dropping back into his previous state. He seemed to sleep for a while. At one time he sat up and yelled, "Pirates." Only the helmsman and a couple of watch standers heard him. At 6am Captain Murphy came to see how he was doing and watched as Silas and Ed Smith gave him his medicine. He was given another cold water wash down while the Captain stood beside him.

Captain Murphy told Silas and Ed he was very appreciative of the care and time the crew members were devoting to Andy's welfare during his fever. "I will make note of it in the ship's log and place a letter in all personnel files. It may help if any of them ever try for a commission to officer status."

"I am sure the men do it because they have such high regard for the fine young man Andy is turning into. They all like him," Silas said.

"That's good to hear from you, Silas. It is especially pleasing to know one of my brother's children is making such a favorable impression here on the Java Sea. If there are any changes in his condition please let me know immediately. Also have John Simmons drop in my office today. I want to talk to him about possible reactions to the medicine."

"Yes, sir," Silas replied. "Simmons will be sleeping late today, he had the midnight watch."

The Captain went back to his office. Silas went back to the bo's'n locker. Various members of the crew checked on Andy during the morning as he slept a little more restfully. On his way to the Captain's office, John Simmons stopped to check on Andy and as he was looking him over, Andy screamed. "He's got a sword. He's got a sword."

John placed his hand reassuringly on Andy's shoulder and he quieted down and closed his eyes as if to sleep. He then sat straight up in the makeshift bed and asked, "Why is a pirate like Jack Boldenman walking around the Java Sea?" He fell back on the bed and slept again.

Mac came in the early afternoon with some broth he had made from a lean piece of salt pork. He also had a small cup of pureed peaches from a box he opened for the crew's lunch. The lean salt pork had been soaked several times to get the excess salt out of it, leaving only the lean meat. He and John Simmons gently propped Andy up on the edge of the bed and slowly fed him some of the food. He acted like he was interested in eating, but so weak he had to struggle. John remarked, "He seems to feel a little cooler. Maybe the fever is breaking."

Mac felt his forehead and around his chest area. "I don't know. He feels just the same to me."

The two sailors managed to nurse almost half a cup of broth into Andy and all but a couple of swallows of the pureed peaches. Andy was still in a half-sleep. He wasn't cognizant of his whereabouts or who was attending him. He lay back down and went back into his semi-conscious state. This was the seventh day of his fever and everyone was ill at ease because it was still lingering with no definite sign of breaking. He just lay there quietly all afternoon. At suppertime he got another dose of medicine and some more of Mac's pork broth. This time there was no peaches. Still in his half-sleep state, Andy asked, "Where's the peaches?"

Willie Wispor was helping Mac with the feeding chore and excitedly said, "Did you hear that?"

"You bet I heard it. Andy, I have to go back to the galley to get them. I'll be back in a minute or two," Mac told him.

Sitting, with eyes closed, very weakly Andy started talking to Willie. "I feel pretty sick. I'm awful hungry. My medicine tastes terrible. Somebody gave me some food. Where did the pirates go? Am I still on the Java Sea? Can I have a drink of water?"

With tears in his eyes, old tough man Willie Wispor realized there was a good chance Andy's fever had broken and he was going to be all right with rest and some healthy care. "This is still the Java Sea. I don't know about any pirates. When Mac comes back, I will go get you some water. It's good to see you sitting up and coming out of your fever. You'll have to take it real easy until you get your strength back. I have been doing the cabin boy job sometimes. There is a lot of work to do, at odd hours, in that job. I wouldn't want to do it every day. Here comes Mac with your peaches. I'll go get the water."

Mac fed him the pureed peaches. You could tell he really liked them and ate quickly as Mac fed him. He sat with his eyes closed, groaning in a soft purring sound. Mac asked, "Are you beginning to feel a little better?"

Andy replied, "Uh huh."

Mac finished feeding him the peaches and Willie gave him a small drink of the water. Mac said, "You just lay back and rest. We want you to get well and you need to take it easy for a few days."

When his cold water wash down was finished, Willie told Mac, "I think I will sit with him for a while and check his fever again after he has had a chance to dry off and warm up."

Andy suddenly opened his eyes, looked at Mac and Willie and said, "Where did that pirate go?" He then lay back down with his eyes closed tightly and immediately dropped off to sleep.

Willie and Mac sat talking for a few minutes about Andy's interest in some mythical pirate. Willie remembered having Andy call him Jack one time a day or two ago. It didn't make much of an impression on Willie. Neither he, nor Mac could figure out why Andy talked about pirates.

The Java Sea had been moving slowly toward Recife for the last five days. The wind was so weak it nearly had them becalmed. Lt. Brown told Silas they covered only twenty six miles one day. "The last twenty-four hours we have moved thirty-nine miles closer. We need a good breeze."

"It will come in a few days," Silas said. "Here at the mouth of the Amazon ships have been becalmed forty or fifty days at a time. It is usually for much shorter periods. How far is Recife now?"

"This morning's calculations show us to be eighty miles from the north entrance to the harbor. With a good breeze we could be in there tomorrow, with ease."

"Even at this reduced speed of thirty-nine miles a day, we'll make it in two days. Unless, of course, the arithmetic from this old bo's'n mate's head is wrong," Silas told him, adding a little chuckle because he knew he was trying to be humorous and tease Lt. Brown.

The Lieutenant told Silas, "I sure hope you're right about the wind picking up. Navigation is very boring when you are making less than forty miles a day." He then added the same sound of chuckle Silas had added.

John Simmons came up and gave Andy his evening dose of medicine. Andy acted like he was sleeping right through the procedure. He made a face but lay down and went back to sleep. John felt him in several places to check his temperature. He sat a few minutes and checked him again. After doing it for the third time he left and went to the Captain's office. He reported to Captain Murphy on Andy's condition.

"Captain Murphy, I believe Andy has passed the peak of his fever and is on the way back to good health, providing of course, he doesn't have some kind of relapse. I think he was extremely sick and may have repercussions years from now. I think the tree limb scrapings were the prime thing aiding his recovery. The care and compassion he receives from all members of the crew of the Java Sea is exceptionally good also. I hope and pray he continues to improve. He is a good boy."

"Thank you, John. It certainly takes a load off my mind to hear your report. As you know, Andy is my nephew. About five years ago I told him he could be my cabin boy at age twelve. He never forgot. When he neared twelve years he came looking for the job. From my end, he has worked out well."

The two men sensed they were deeply concerned about Andy and shook hands before saying, 'Good night.' John passed by Andy's bunk as he headed to his own. Andy was sleeping well and seemed to be a little cooler to the touch.

At four-twenty, Rosco Quinn, who had taken the helmsman watch at four o'clock, noticed the main sail was beginning to build a small bulge indicating a slight breeze was holding steady. He checked the compass bearings to be sure the ship was holding to the course set by Captain Murphy before he retired at eleven o'clock. As the sun peeked over the horizon, the topsails and gallants filled, moving the ship enough those on deck could feel movement in the air. Within an hour the speed of the Java Sea was noticeable to the crew coming on deck to start their day.

Silas came into the wheelhouse and asked Rosco how long ago the ship started moving with the wind coming in on her port quarter. When he was told it happened an hour and fifteen minutes ago he decided to order the sails set at a different angle to catch more of the wind and make it easier to hold her on her course toward Recife. He then went to the chow hall and told his deck crewmen what they would do as soon as breakfast was finished.

"I want the climbers to bring in the studding sail gear from the port side as soon as the main sails are clear. We will have that side against the dock in Recife. There is no sense leaving our studding gear out where it may get broken during loading and off loading. All those assigned to the deck will check for any fouled lines and take in the main sails on all three masts when the order is given. The sky sails, royals and gallants will come down when called. Remember, keep your mind on what you are doing and think about safety as the first order of work. Are there any questions?"

One of the sailors in the back of the chow hall asked, "Are we going to have any time to go ashore and see the town?"

Silas laughed out loud, and said, "I knew it, I knew it. That's always been the first question at a work session when there are new sailors aboard. As far as I know, at this time I will say yes there will be time ashore in Recife. I must also tell you we will be spending time in Rio de Janeiro, Montevideo and Buenos Aires before we head back north. Don't buy all your gifts or spend all your money in the first port you go ashore."

As Silas talked to the men, Captain Murphy and Lt. Brown came in and sat in a corner of the chow hall to have their breakfast. Captain Murphy spoke to Silas, "Can I have a word with the crew when you are finished, Silas?"

"Yes Sir, Captain Murphy. In fact you can start right now. All we are doing is questions and answers at this point. I have already given them their work instructions for entering Recife."

The Captain stood up and said, "Thank you, Silas." Turning to the men he addressed them about the policy of the shipping company regarding pay in foreign ports. "Gentlemen, I heard some of the talk about going ashore in Recife. It's my duty as Captain to oversee the operation of the Java Sea as a profitable venture for the company and the investors who own the ship. You and I do the work necessary to deliver the cargoes they provide at the ports on our list of places to visit. They in turn pay and provide living conditions aboard the ship. The policy of the company is to allow a sailor to withdraw one half of his accrued pay when entering a port of call, if he so desires.

"The reason for this one-half pay withdrawal procedure has come from experiences the company has had over several years. At first the company let sailors take all their pay at any time. The sailors went ashore in strange ports and were robbed or spent all their money buying local merchandise. This left them broke and having to start from zero to accumulate a new bankroll. They also jumped ship with their pockets full of their earnings, leaving the company with a ship needing a crew. The half pay procedure makes it possible for the sailor to have money, and with the same amount left behind on the ship's books, he is inclined to come back aboard. In the long run, this policy works well for both parties.

"Now, I'll ask you the same question Silas did. Are there any questions?"

CHAPTER 19

▼

Although it was light, the breeze was enough to bring the ship into port in early afternoon and the crew made preparations to offload the cargo. Everything consigned to Recife would be unloaded the next day.

With two hours of daylight remaining, Silas had the crew stop working and allowed them to go into town. There was one main street about 400 yards long, Recife was not an impressive port of call. The sailors walked up and down the one street, looking in windows. The stores were filled with home made merchandise of native origin. They found many shops containing jewelry and trinkets for women and girls. It was easy to see they catered to sailors from visiting ships whose crews bought presents for wives and sweethearts at home.

Some of the Java Sea sailors ventured into the stores and found the best merchandise was located in the middle of the store surrounded by a lesser quality of native creations being offered. When asked why all the good things were displayed behind the inferior products, the owner, in broken English replied, "Must keep things safe. Natives from jungle take without paying. You need help, we help you. Plenty stuff here. You buy."

Rosco Quinn tapped Ed Smith on the shoulder and said, "You see Ed, not all shoplifters come from big cities, some are still in the jungle."

"Yeah, but some of our big cities are also getting to be like jungles," Ed replied.

"Do you think it is getting worse in the city or the jungle," Rosco asked?

"I wouldn't be surprised if the city turns into a jungle with all the people moving there looking for work. The bad guys will move right along with everyone else. It will take a few more years, but you mind my word, our cities are going to be full of crooks. How can anyone survive in a city today without stealing and cheating?"

"You sound worried, Ed."

"I am worried. I hate to think of our cities being overrun by people without decency and purpose in their lives. We need ethical people running our cities, and states too?"

They had been walking along the street while talking and met Lt. Brown, Silas and Willie Wispor. They each had a present for Andy. He was still too sick to come ashore. Willie had bought him three pair of earrings, explaining if Andy kept talking about pirates he might like his own earring. If he doesn't want one, he can give them to his mother and two sisters. Lt. Brown had a book on navigation and Silas had some soft cotton underwear. Rosco and Ed decided to look for something to take back to Andy. Ed decided on a small bundle of sugar cane a street vendor was selling. Rosco bought him a book of short stories.

Everyone came back aboard a little before sundown and Mac served some snacks in lieu of a full supper. He promised a breakfast of meat and eggs with fried potatoes. When asked where he got the fresh meat, eggs and potatoes, he replied, "While all of you were having fun in town, the five of us who stayed with the ship bought them from a vendor who came along side in a small sailboat with an outrigger. I also got a few fresh oranges for Andy and a bottle of cooking oil that has spices mixed in it."

Andy was asleep as the crew came back. The many gifts they had purchased for him were left beside his bed and the man on watch was told to make sure they stayed put until Andy awoke and could see them. He was given another dose of his medicine by Silas and John. They both thought his temperature was lower. In fact, he no longer felt overly hot.

"We should have the Captain write a letter to Captain Fleming on the Marie Luce thanking him for the medicine for Andy, letting him know Andy is improving," John suggested.

Silas agreed it was a good idea. He thought it would be best to wait until Andy gained some of his strength back. "I am sure Captain Murphy will be happy to write a thank you letter to Captain Fleming. Perhaps he could write it as a thank you note from the crew of the Java Sea. I think that would be welcome by Captain Fleming. What do you think?"

"I'm with you all the way. I think it an excellent idea to have Captain Murphy write a letter," John said.

Two days later the Java Sea moved away from the dock and into an anchorage, awaiting wind and tidal currents to take her out of the harbor and back into the

Atlantic Ocean. There, she would set a course due south for the next two-hundred miles, before making daily south-south-west corrections to bring her into Rio de Janeiro. Winds were sporadic and light in the latitudes they were now sailing. Near the equator it was always hot. Two weeks slipped past before anyone noticed a slight cooling trend to the weather.

Andy continued to improve. The crew worked to take care of him, almost as much as they did when he was in the midst of the worst days of his fever. It took him three days to gather enough strength to stand alone and two more to take a few normal steps. For the next week he struggled to walk on the deck. He said it was harder to become reacquainted to the pitch than the sideways roll. As his strength returned he worked harder to get back to where he had been before the fever. The crew admired his fortitude and all offered to help him go from place to place when he was walking along a deck.

By the end of the third week he was doing well and John Simmons said, "I think he is cured. He will have to watch what he does and take a dose of his medicine at the first sign of any relapse. He should not overdo for at least two more months. Fever is one of many things we do not know much about after effects."

The Java Sea was in and out of rain squalls every day now. Some days there were as many as twenty-five small squalls to hit the vessel. One morning a large squall came on them from astern. With expert ship handling, the crew kept the ship in the squall long enough to increase her speed and stay with the squall as it headed south-south-west. Navigational records show the ship covered eighteen miles during the hour and a half she was able to stay with the squall. Everyone liked the idea of getting to Rio at a faster pace.

"We should pray for big squalls," said Rosco.

"A man should be careful what he prays for, because he might get more than he wants," retorted Willie Wispor.

Andy laughed at Willie's cutting remark to Rosco. "Could praying for a large squall bring a hurricane?" he asked.

"I suppose," Willie replied. "We don't need one of those."

Still heading a few compass points west of south the ship continued on its way toward Rio de Janeiro. Work was routine. Andy tried to swing himself up into the shrouds and ratlines. He couldn't get his feet to swing more than a foot above the deck. John Simmons saw him trying and told him not to do it for at least another month. He told him there would be plenty of time to climb the rigging after he got his strength completely back.

The lack of a busy routine, with considerable work to do, had Andy deeply bored as the days came, and went. His only jobs seemed to be carrying coffee to the officers at 5:30 each morning and cleaning vegetables for Mac. Because they had not been in a port in over three weeks, the only vegetable cleaning was carrots and potatoes. He faithfully peeled potatoes and scraped carrots nearly every day.

The Java Sea was leaving a good wake behind her. The sails were taught in a stiff breeze. The sound of rigging stretching and relaxing to the rhythm of the breeze, overpowered once in a while as the bowsprit dipped headlong, deep into the next wave. Otherwise it was quiet above decks as Andy walked across the after deck toward officers' quarters, with two cups of coffee on a tray. It was still dark, with a slight hint of light on the eastern horizon.

Suddenly there was a loud crack, like the sound of a gun going off. Andy jumped, spilling much of the coffee. It was followed by a crashing sound coming from the fo'c'sle deck. He turned around and went to the galley to get more coffee and clean the tray. He told Mac, "Something happened to the rigging on the foremast. Part of it came crashing to the deck. We better wake Silas."

"You should not worry about it, the night watch will wake him if they haven't already," Mac told him. "Say, haven't you got the coffee down to the Captain and Lieutenant, yet?"

"I was on my way there when the rigging broke and startled me. I spilled coffee in the tray. This is fresh coffee I am taking to them now."

As Andy headed back to officers quarters with the replenished coffee he noticed there was a lot more light showing in the eastern sky. He turned to look toward the foremast. He couldn't see what happened in the dim dawn light other than a jumble of rigging draped from the fo'c'sle deck down to the main deck. He continued on his way to deliver the coffee.

Entering the chart room, between the two officer's rooms, he was greeted with a hearty welcome by both men. "What happened to make you a little later than usual with coffee this morning, Andy?" asked Captain Murphy.

"Something let go on the foremast, I jumped and spilled the first tray of coffee. This coffee, I went back to the galley to replace what I spilled. I had to clean the tray and get fresh cups." Andy replied.

"Do you know what let go on the foremast?"

"No sir, Captain Murphy. Some of it came down on the fo'c'sle deck and is hanging down to the main deck. I didn't go close to it and didn't see it well in the dim light of dawn. Silas should be up there now. Do you want me to go ask him what happened and come back and tell you?"

"That won't be necessary Andy. Lt. Brown and I will be going to the chow hall for breakfast in a few minutes and we can check on it at that time. Thank you for the coffee. That will be all for now. On second thought I do have a special chore I've been keeping on the back of the stove, so to speak. Will you come back about 10 o'clock and I'll show you what has to be done?"

"Yes sir, Captain Murphy."

Andy went up on the main deck and walked forward to see what happened to the rigging. Silas was there with a crew of five men. They were picking up and coiling the running lines of the skysail. It had let go and came crashing to the deck when the skysail yard broke in half. A quick glance over the mess told him it was going to require some sail sewing and line splicing to get it back in working condition. Somehow they would have to get a new yardarm for the skysail up and attached to the foremast where the broken one had been. The skysail was torn in several places. It would require at least a day of sewing to repair it and put it in working order. Two of the jibs had tears in them and the metal strap around a double pulley was badly bent. Only the blacksmith would be able to repair it by heating and bending it back to its original shape.

After watching the crew for a couple of minutes, Andy asked Silas, "Can I help with any of the splicing and sewing to help you get it back in working shape? I'm free until 10 o'clock when I have to go do something for Captain Murphy."

"You sure can. Take these two coils of line and put them together with a tapered splice about eight inches long. Once you're finished, coil it, bring it back, and I'll give you more to splice. When everything is spliced we will start sewing sails. Everyone will be working on this after we get the deck cleared."

Captain Murphy and Lt. Brown came to talk to Silas before they went to breakfast. Captain Murphy wanted to know if Silas had all the necessary spare parts he needed to restore the damage to working order. Assured by Silas the only thing he was uncertain of at this time is the condition of the pulleys on the upper mast. "I believe they are alright, when we pulled the broken lines out of them, they appeared free enough to be in working order," He said to the Captain and Lieutenant. "We will know more about what it's going to require for a new sky-sail in another half hour," he added.

"I am confident in the hands of this capable crew, under your direction, we will be up and running in shorter time than other ships of the company, under similar circumstances. We are fortunate to have such a good crew of men on one vessel." Captain Murphy told him.

"Can I have Andy for a half hour about 8:30 this morning?" the Lieutenant asked.

"Anytime, Lieutenant," Silas replied. "The more the boy learns about your job, the better it is for his future, if he's going to follow a career at sea."

"Thank you Silas. He is doing well and learning fast. I hope the sickness didn't set him back too far. I'll be able to get an idea of what he has retained, after we do a few navigational readings this week. He is a smart young man."

"Will one of you tell him he doesn't have to come to my office this morning? The job I have can wait until tomorrow, or another day, as long as it's finished before we go into Rio," Captain Murphy said to Lt. Brown and Silas.

CHAPTER 20

▼

Andy knocked on the Captain's door. When he was told to come in, he opened the door and said, "Captain Murphy, I am here to do the special job you asked me to come back for. Is now a good time to start on it?"

"Sit down Andy and I will be with you in a couple of minutes. I am making a report on yesterday's equipment failure. You may be able to add something as you were the one present when it happened. I believe Silas and the crew have it all repaired. The only problem, as I understand it, was getting the new yardarm from the hold and into place on the mast. It seems they had to move a lot of cargo to get to where the extra yardarms are stored."

Lt. Brown, who had been sitting quietly at his desk while Andy and Captain Murphy talked, said, "It looks like this accident with the skysail yard breaking and the problem of retrieving the spare from the hold has taught us a lesson. We are going to recommend to the head office that all spare yards be carried, lashed in a convenient place. There is plenty of room under the rails, both inboard and outboard. I will ask you to help me measure the prospective storage places once I have retrieved all yardarm measures from our blueprints. We'll have to find safe secure places to store them. The foremast and mizzenmast have duplicate yards so we will have to store only one set as backup."

Captain Murphy got up from his desk and brought a large stack of papers to the chart table. The sheets were all the same except for color. There seemed to be pink, yellow and white sheets in the pile he laid down. "Come over here Andy and I will show you what needs to be done. These are the papers that were blown all over the room when the windows and portholes were left open. They need to be sorted out and put in numerical order. The lowest number is 00,001. The highest number will be 06,248. They are a combined bill of laden and shipping order for cargo the Java Sea has handled since I last sent the paperwork to the main office. I must have them in order when I visit a main office in Rio.

"I'll do the best I can," Andy said. "Can I start now?"

"I think you will want to sort them on the chart table. If Lt. Brown isn't going to use the table you can start now."

"He can have the chart table as long as he wants it this week. I am working on logarithm tables for the longitudes and latitudes we will need from here to Buenos Aires."

Andy looked through the pile of papers and thought about the best way to work on them to collate the whole pile. He thought of his sister Maria and what she had taught the children in school about putting things in order by number. He decided to make three smaller piles with each of the three colors in separate piles. He finished before lunch and placed one of Lt. Brown's Navigational books on each pile to hold it in place.

After lunch he decided he would start on the white pile first. He knew there are numbers from zero to nine in each column of sheet numbers. He sorted to get everything in the hundreds place in order, making ten piles. He would sort each pile to the next numerical place and have ten more piles. This, he decided, would put him in position to collate according to the right hand number on the sheet, leaving him with all sheets in the piles needing to be put in order to have everything collated.

By the end of the day he had the white sheets sorted to the hundredth position numerically. The following morning he started working on the white sheet again. By noon time he had almost put the white sheets in order. He worked with Lt. Brown on the daily noontime position of the ship, before going back to the collating work. The following morning he had all the white sheets in numerical order and had the yellow sheets spread out according to the third, or middle, number. He was getting faster at handling the paper and quickly spotting the number.

Two days later he took all the sheets back to Captain Murphy's desk and told him they were all in order. "That's a great job Andy. You did it very quickly. I appreciate it, thank you."

Andy tried swinging his feet up to the shrouds as he headed for the galley to talk to Mac. He managed to do it, but not as easy as he had before the fever. He decided to keep trying, continuing to work on getting his strength back. The galley was empty except for Mac. He was mixing some flour for pie crust. He was planning to make a pot pie for the evening meal with a large grouper Rosco

Quinn had caught on a drag line. He asked Andy if he felt like helping him cut up some vegetables. When Andy replied, "Sure," Mac went into the storage bin and brought back potatoes, beets, carrots and parsnips.

When they started peeling the vegetables, Andy asked, "Mac, can I ask you some questions about Jack Boldenman?"

"Yes. But, who is Jack Boldenman?"

"You mean you don't know him. He came aboard the Java Sea. I think he is a friend of my uncle, Captain Murphy."

"When did he come aboard here?"

"I think it was three to four weeks ago, when I was sick on the poop deck, behind the wheelhouse. He talked to me. He was here several days."

"First off, I never heard of him and there wasn't anyone who came aboard while you were sick."

"But, he's a pirate and knows Captain Murphy. They're friends. He talked to me several times and told me he had a lot of treasure hidden away."

"Andy, lad, this conversation is never going to go anywhere, because I never heard of a Jack Boldenman and nobody came aboard the Java Sea while you were sick. I think you should talk to your uncle, Captain Murphy or discuss it with John Simmons who gave you the wood scrapings medicine from Captain Fleming. John might know something."

Andy let the subject drop. He asked Mac what size pieces he wanted the vegetables cut into? He cut the potatoes he had peeled and dropped them into the large kettle Mac placed on the table where they worked. Mac scraped the carrots and parsnips. They worked on the few beets together.

With the vegetables prepared Mac told Andy he could leave and suggested he go take a rest in the crew's quarters. "I think you still have some healing to do."

He went looking for John Simmons and found him painting the waist on the fo'c'sle. "Can I talk to you while you work?" He asked.

"I think so, as long as you don't complain about my painting!" John replied in jest.

Andy asked him, "Do you know a pirate named Jack Boldenman?"

"I never heard of him. Why do you ask?"

"I think he may be a friend of my uncle, Captain Murphy. I believe I saw him on this ship. I believe the Java Sea aided him in hiding a treasure. I believe everyone is trying to keep it a secret from me. I'd like to tell someone what I know."

"Go ahead and tell me about it, I'll just keep painting and listen."

Andy's Story of Jack Boldenman

"I heard the lookout call out, 'Sail Ho'."

"I dozed off for a few minutes and when I woke up there was a man standing by my hammock I had never seen before. He was a tall rough looking man. He had a big brown moustache with waxed ends sticking out both sides of his face. On his chin he wore a goatee, cut small and hardly noticeable. His pants were more like pantaloons made for an Arabian Nights character, like Sinbad. They were bright yellow with a sky-blue silk shirt hanging loosely over his hips. He wore two pistols at his hips with a large sword hanging under his left hand.

"During the next few days the Pirate came and visited me. I think he knew I didn't like him or trust him. He was always polite and friendly to me. He told me he was a friend of my uncle, Captain Murphy. I didn't believe him and argued with him that my uncle wouldn't be friends with a pirate. He always laughed at me. He said they became friends when a British man-of-war sank his old ship, leaving all hands to drown in the ocean. Uncle Fred found them three days later and rescued them with the loss of only two pirates. Captain Murphy put them ashore in North Africa. They stole a fishing boat and went across the Strait of Gibraltar where they found a British Navy ship manned by two guards, while the crew was ashore celebrating the sinking of two French Navy brigantines near Toulon, France. They boarded the British ship, overpowered the two guards, cut the anchors loose, set sail and stole the ship. It is the ship they are using now. She is an18-gun Warship named Rosebud by the British. The pirates call her Matilda.

"He told me he needed the Java Sea because of her extra tall mainmast. We changed course and sailed for two days in an east southeast direction. We came to three small islands with little vegetation. One was tall and jutted up more than two-hundred feet on its southerly end. There was a cave on a rugged cliff about one hundred feet above the waterline. By rigging off the top of the Java Sea's mainmast, they raised their stolen treasure up and into the cave with ropes and pulleys.

"I couldn't tell how, but they had been up to the cave before. There was a line hanging out of the cave. A pirate caught the line from the top of their mainmast and climbed into the cave. Once there, he lowered the lines to the deck of the Java Sea to be attached on the mainmast top. After the hoisting rigging was in place it only took a few minutes to hoist the fifteen boxes and trunks to the cave. As the pirates pulled around to pick up their man from the cave, we headed away on a southerly course.

"Somewhere east southeast of the Amazon delta is three islands with Pirate Jack Boldenman's treasure, hidden in a cave, on the side of a cliff.

"I doubt I can think of anything additional to tell you about what happened when Jack Bodenman came aboard. I only know I saw it happen and everyone is misleading me to make me think I am crazy or something. Can you help me?"

John was silent for a few minutes as Andy's story ran through his head and he thought about some of the things he learned at Yale. He knew he didn't take the medical courses. He was friendly and talked with many of the medical students. He also listened to their discussions. He decided all indications point toward one or more of three things; reaction from an overdose of medicine, severe fever, or hallucinations.

"Andy, do you know anything about the word hallucination?"

"I've never heard of it before."

"Alright, I'll try to explain it in the best way I can. I think it is the answer to your problem. I am sure we can get to the bottom of it, if we keep trying."

"To begin, you were a very sick boy. You ran an extremely high temperature for many days. The body is not accustomed to being that sick and hot for as long as you were. The result of your sickness could have had an effect on your overall health. You were getting cool down washes on a regular basis. After the first few days a New Bedford whale ship came alongside. The captain, a man from Nova Scotia named Alex Fleming, gave us a piece of tree limb he said would lower your temperature if we boiled fine shavings scraped from the wood and gave you the liquid. On the second day some of us thought you felt cooler to the touch. Not everyone agreed. You eventually cooled down to a normal temperature after five or six days of taking four doses a day of Captain Fleming's cure.

"A sickness, like you just went through, can leave a person with side effects totally unrelated to what might be expected. It's not unusual for a person to have a sort of hangover from some medications. The hangover effect can be anything other than the normal. Have you ever had a dream at night and when you awoke the next day you thought the dream was something that really happened?"

"Yes, at least a couple of times," Andy replied.

"I can only diagnose what you are telling me about the pirates from my knowledge of the tricks a person's brain can play when it's not expected. That's what is called a hallucination. I think the long duration of your fever and the medicine, left you with a hallucination. It will eventually go away. Once you realize there are too many parts to your story of the pirate which could not happen. Captain Murphy would not befriend a pirate, there are no islands in the middle of the Atlantic at those longitudes and latitudes, no one has ever heard of Jack

Boldenman and I doubt the British Navy would leave a gunboat unmanned while the crew went to a party.

"That is the best explanation I can see in this situation. I'm sorry Andy. You are going to have to accept the fact your bad fever and the medicine you were given left you with a wild sea story in your head."

"Are you sure of it?" Andy wanted to know.

"I'm as sure of it as I am sure we are sitting here talking about it."

"Thank you John. I believe you. It was so real, it was so real."

CHAPTER 21

▼

Rio de Janeiro was a teaming place with people rushing around in all directions. There were a lot of different languages being spoken. Spanish and Portuguese seemed to be most common. Andy found several people talking English, even children near his own age. He asked a young boy where he could find a store to buy gifts. "Come, I will show you," he said. "My name is Juan Velho. My family owns a town on the Great Argentina Pampas. We raise cattle and sheep, and have many pastures."

Andy told him, "My name is Andy Murphy. I am cabin boy on the ship Java Sea. I am an American. I grew up on a farm with horses, cattle, chickens, pigs and a few turkeys. We grew much hay and vegetables we sold."

"I saw you get off the big ship and wondered why a boy would be working at such a job. Is it not too dangerous to climb the tall masts to fix the sails?"

"A cabin boy doesn't have to climb the masts unless he is trained to do it before he goes up to the high places," Andy explained. "I'm just learning to climb and will never be assigned to a climbing job until I'm fully recognized and capable of always climbing in a safe manner. I also have to be strong enough. The boatswains mate makes the decision on my ability."

As they talked they were walking toward an area with some buildings taller than Andy had ever seen before. It was the developing retail, residential, hotel and general government area. There was work going on everywhere. On one side of the street they were building a five story hotel and across the street would be a ten story combination Insurance-Bank building, already open and doing business on its ground floor. At the next corner a large retail store was under construction.

Juan led Andy into a large department store with a gift section located on the fourth floor. Andy found things he wanted to take home to his sisters and parents. He told Juan he would come back in the morning with a couple of friends to help him carry them to the ship. First he must find out if he could have space large enough on the Java Sea to store a small bureau. He could keep all the other things in the bureau.

The two boys, led by Juan, went to the beach and after rolling up their pant legs, walked along the edge of the water in the soft sand. They talked about working with farm animals. Juan said, "I don't like horses, cattle, saddle sores, open fire cooking, dirt, dust, sleeping in the rain and I couldn't throw the bola. I'm not meant to be a gaucho."

"I liked the farm work at my home," Andy said. "We had two nice, gentle cows and the large draft horses are gentle creatures. I didn't work on a cattle ranch, I worked on a farm. We raised many different kinds of vegetables to sell."

"In America, could I find a job?"

"If you want to work, you can find a job. You can't get paid to stand around or sleep all day. People have to work and produce a product or service to get paid. There is no featherbed in America. We're building a country there. You should expect to work."

"You will take me there on your ship if I work to pay my way?"

"You'll have to ask the Captain. You can come down to the dock and ask him in the morning. We are not leaving for two days."

"It is time to go back. We have many steps to make before we are back to beginning of our journey to here," Juan said.

When Andy got back to the ship he went to the galley and talked to Mac about what he had bought as presents for his family. When he asked about storing them on the ship until they got home, Mac told him it would be up to the Captain. Silas came in a few minutes later and he told Andy only the Captain can decide about extra large gifts crew members want to take home. He asked them who could help him bring the things from the store and was told it would be necessary to get someone to deliver them to the dock.

Andy was sure Captain Murphy would give him permission to store the bureau and gifts behind the Chart table. He would need a helper to bring them from the store and watch them while he brought them aboard a piece at a time. The crew would be busy offloading cargo for the next two days. He would have to arrange something with Juan Velho.

Captain Murphy approved Andy bringing the gifts aboard and storing them behind the chart table if it would not interfere with Lt. Brown and his work. Lt.

Brown indicated it would not be in his way, "I seldom go behind the table," he said.

Andy found Juan waiting on the dock the next morning, all excited about asking Captain Murphy for a job to pay his passage to America. The discussion with Captain Murphy didn't last long. Juan was willing to agree to all conditions that would give him passage to America. Juan believed he would be happy as an assistant cabin boy to his new friend Andy. The papers were drawn up by Lt. Brown. Captain Murphy and Lt. Brown were extremely surprised when Juan read the papers and signed them in a graceful longhand.

"Where did you learn to speak English?" Andy asked him.

"We had a school on the ranch. A teacher named Mr. McHale from Ireland taught there. He showed us how to read and write in English."

Andy and Juan left to get the bureau and gifts. The store agreed to pack the gifts in the bureau draws and deliver everything on the dock in the afternoon. With a receipt in hand, written in Spanish and approved by Juan, the two headed back to the Java Sea to let Juan get acquainted with shipboard life and people. "We must stop at my home to get my things on the way to the ship."

"We need to hurry because I want to be there when the store brings my things. I want to bring them aboard without the crew having to work on them. They were good enough to me while I was sick."

They ventured up a narrow alley and at the end of the row of buildings were some scrap wood, sheet metal and cardboard attached in lean-to fashion big enough for a person to crawl in and lie down on the earthen floor. Beside it was another scrap-built storage space about the size of a small steamer trunk. Juan opened it and took out a few clothes, a magazine and a pair of extra shoes. He crawled in the sleeping section and came out with a burlap grain sack which he used to carry the clothes. He threw the sack over his shoulder and went around to the front of the house. A knock on the door brought a young woman with a baby in her arms and the question in Spanish, "What do you want?"

"I'm leaving," Juan told her. "I have a new job. I'm the assistant cabin boy on the big ship Java Sea. Tell your husband he can have my machete and my bola. I will not need them as a cabin boy. Thank him for letting me have a place to stay. Adios.

They arrived at the ship about the same time the crew finished the day's offloading. They found Silas, and after introductions were ended, made arrangements for a berth for Juan. Juan could hardly believe his living conditions were so remarkably improved. "I never had such a nice place to sleep after I left the ranch, until right now," he said.

Mac was not overjoyed at having a new cabin boy to train until he realized most of Juan's training would be Andy's responsibility. He asked Juan, "Do you speak and understand good English?"

"Yes, Senor, if you speak good English I'll know what you are saying. I can read and write also in your American way."

Mac went silent. He was not able to read and write easily. Only the shipboard forms he was familiar with came easy. A new writing was out of the question. He couldn't read it. "All right," he said, "you will be a new cabin boy and assistant to Andy for this voyage. You be sure and do what Andy and I tell you to do and there will be no problems. Andy is a good cabin boy with nine month's experience. He works hard, you must work hard. Understand?"

"Yes, sir."

Rosco Quinn walked in and told Andy there was a team on the dock with a piece of furniture addressed to him. Andy and Juan went topside to oversee the unloading. On the dock they found two men with a horse team and the bureau already unloaded. The two boys checked for scratches and finding none, started to sign off on the drover's copy of the shipment from the store. "Don't sign anything until you look in the draws for the gifts," Rosco told them. "These guys help themselves to other people's things sometimes."

Everything was there. Andy signed. To make it easy, Silas and Rosco hoisted the bureau and its contents onto the ship, setting it on the number two hatch cover where it would be handy for moving below decks to the navigational office.

The next day the crew loaded several wagon loads of lumber and some boxes of wool jackets with wool pants hanging full length in special containers. They were consigned to stores in New York City. Andy spent the day training Juan in his new job. He was a little awkward in handling dishes and especially a tray with coffee cups. He didn't spill anything. He came close several times. Only his nimble body and acute sense of balance saved the day. He was a willing, hard worker. Both Silas and Lt. Brown noticed how well he worked under Andy's direction. While Andy was with Lt. Brown, Juan and Mac worked on the galley chores with Mac later remarking, "That new kid is a good worker. He's kind of all thumbs, but he'll learn."

Once late evening came and they were free for the balance of the day, the two boys went to the fo'c'sle and watched the sun set over the city of Rio de Janeiro. They talked about Juan's first full day as a cabin boy assistant. He was not sure he would like the job on a full time basis. He would rather have a little more free time. "Working is for slaves and hired gauchos," he mumbled.

"Oh, no," Andy told him, "working is for people who want to make an honest living and leave a good mark on the world."

"Well, who wants to do this kind of work?"

"You do, if you want to get to America."

"I could find another way."

"What other way? The only way is by ship. Do you have enough money to buy a ship, or a ticket on a ship?"

"I'll think about it. First, I'll work with you to earn my way there."

"At this point in time, I think that is your best decision."

The next morning, Mac woke the boys just before four o'clock. They washed and headed for the galley. Juan stumbled over his wash bucket and Andy accused him of sleep walking. Juan showed a sensitive side Andy hadn't seen before. He made a mental note that Juan doesn't joke about things, especially if he is on the receiving end of a tease. Juan took the coffee to the officers while Andy set tables and placed silverware and coffee mugs. He went into the galley to help Mac with breakfast. He was told to break eggs into a large kettle so they could be dipped with a ladle for cooking scrambled eggs with precooked bacon chopped up in them.

"Juan seems to be catching on, but is a little slow at what he does around the galley," Mac said.

"He's never worked at this kind of job before. In fact, I don't know what kinds of work he has had experience on other than he was born and raised on a big ranch in Argentina, worked as a gaucho and didn't like it. Quit and came to Rio about a year ago."

By noon the cargo was loaded and the crew was eating their lunch. Captain Murphy came into the chow hall and told everyone we would be getting underway as soon as we could get sail up. "We are picking up an offshore breeze and the tide will be going out in two hours," he told them. "Our next stop will be Montevideo, Uruguay. If all goes well we should make it in about a week. We will then go to Buenos Aires where we will lay over for Christmas and New Year holidays. After we are loaded there we will head north with stops at Rio de Janeiro, Salvador and Recife. Some of our northbound cargo is destined for Portugal and England. Our stops will be Lisbon, Portugal and Plymouth, England. From there we will head back across the Atlantic, stopping in Nova Scotia, Canada to take advantage of the low drain tides. We will careen the ship to make a repair below the waterline. If anyone wants to resign before we complete this voyage, please do so at a port where additional help can be hired as replacement. I thank you all and appreciate your efforts as a crew for the Java Sea."

Captain Murphy walked over and sat down at a table with Silas and Lt. Brown. He didn't have time to pick up his napkin before Juan was standing at his side with coffee and a kettle of hot stew. A ladle protruding from its top was nearly hidden by the steam. "It looks like I am getting some hot lunch here today. Thank you, Juan. You're doing a good job under Andy's direction."

"Thank you, Captain Murphy, Sir."

CHAPTER 22

▼

As the Java Sea came out of Rio de Janeiro into the open sea, the sun was heading down toward the western horizon. The great ship picked up speed under full sail, including studding sails which were set along with all standard sails. The afternoon watch had the helm. All the sails were taught, not straining. Andy told Juan, "Sailing like this will keep the crew and Silas happy. Nothing will get ripped to shreds in this breeze."

Just before daybreak there was a noticeable increase in the wind speed. Sails were adjusted to take advantage of the wind. With the ship on a port tack, she was making more knots than on any day since leaving Baltimore in May. The seas were running heavier and the ship was pitching and rolling more. Juan began to feel the motion and asked Andy where he should go to throw up his breakfast. "You're sea sick from the movements of the ship. Your best place to stay is down on the second deck near the mainmast. That's the center of the pitching and rolling. There is less movement there. I'll have Mac make you some special tea to ease the urges making you sick," Andy told him.

The strong wind and heavy seas stayed with them for two days. After it cleared, Lt. Brown and Andy took a position and found they had covered 528 miles in the last two days. The Java Sea had been sailing with a squall both days, moving south-south-west at an average speed of eleven miles and hour. As word got around the ship all the old timers said a ship like the Java Sea could not move that fast over such a long time period. Andy and Lt. Brown disagreed. As navigators, they had double checked their position readings several times, finding no errors in the calculations. As the squall moved ahead, the ship slowed to nine and then six knots.

NOTE:

By sailing before the strong wind squall on their way to Montevideo, Captain Murphy and the crew of the Java Sea set a record of four and a half days sailing time between the two ports. The record is still unbroken by a sailing ship. Even the faster, tall Clipper ships of the late1800s did not break her record. It is the one and only speed record the Java Sea holds, the only reason she is remembered.

The following day a course correction was made toward the southwest. Soon the crew was sighting familiar land jutting out of the ocean. Again, it was the old timers who said, 'we are not far from Montevideo, the coastline is familiar.'

Juan began to feel better and his stomach problems eased enough for him to eat some soda crackers. Other crew members, who had been through a siege of sea sickness, sympathized with him. John Simmons told him, "That is the only sickness I have ever had that made me want to die. I hope you never have it again."

At Montevideo all docks were in use. The Java Sea had to wait her turn at a mooring buoy in the harbor. Three days later she was warped into a dock where she would remain until she finished unloading and loading of holds number one and three. Securing the cargo to ride well in heavy seas took extra time. It was destined for Lisbon, Portugal and Plymouth, England. Andy and Juan were busy carrying water to the hard working crew. Breaks for meals were on a half crew on, half crew off basis to keep the work moving. It took ten days to complete, with a crew worn out by the fourteen hour days.

With the ship loaded Captain Murphy decided to remain tied to the dock for two more days as a rest time for the crew. Andy and Juan went ashore and walked around the town. Andy bought three hand-woven belts for his mother and two sisters. He picked three different colors, all the same size, deciding they could decide the one they wanted, when he brought them home.

It took four days for the Java Sea to move from Montevideo up the Rio de la Plata, Uruguay to Buenos Aires, Argentina. It was six days before Christmas and festivities were already started. Religious statuary was placed at all street intersections, on buildings and in front of every store in the large business area. Starting on the twentieth of December there were parades held each day, including Christmas morning. Juan became the tour guide for the sailors as they went ashore in groups. He explained decorations and the meaning of signs painted in Spanish or Portuguese. He helped them shop for gifts and personal items. He was at home in Argentina, becoming a gracious host to his shipmates.

Two days before Christmas Andy and Juan had gone ashore with Ed Smith and William Isley to help them shop in some of the smaller stores. On Necochea Street the foursome entered a small store with an elderly man, its proprietor, as the only clerk available to do business. Prices were extremely high compared with other stores they had shopped in the past two days. They huddled to discuss it and discovered the old man understood their English. He came over to where they were talking and asked, "Where are you men from?"

When they replied they were from an American ship in the harbor, he said, "The prices marked on the goods in this store are marked high to keep the Germans and French out. They hate high prices. They trade elsewhere. I will sell you anything in the store cheaper than you can buy in any other store in Buenos Aires. I will treat my American friends well."

Juan asked him the price of a sheepskin jacket and was told, "Not you, you are a native son of Argentina."

"How do you know," Juan asked?

"I know your father and mother, they are my very good customers and my wife is your mother's sister. Why are you with these American sailors?"

"I am going to America on their ship. I left the ranchero two years past and have been living in Montevideo. My friend Andy here is rescuing me to go to America to be a farmer on a big farm."

"Does your father know this?"

"Yes," Juan lied to his uncle.

Everyone bought something in the store. Juan came out with the largest package having purchased a sheepskin coat. When asked why he had bought a sheepskin coat with the weather so hot, he replied, "I think ahead to America."

The men were happy and sang Christmas Carols much of the day on Christmas. A few of them traded presents and treated the cabin boys to a bag of treats. Captain Murphy purchased a shave, haircut and bath for every man, at the barbershop three blocks away, near the end of the dock. "I thought you may want to get clean before you head for home," he said with a big chuckle, receiving a rousing laugh and a "Yeah, Yeah" in return. Several of the crew sang out, "Thank You, Captain Murphy."

During the week between holidays, some odd pieces of freight were loaded, consigned to various towns in the countries where the Java Sea would make port calls. One piece headed for Spain caught Andy's eye because of the artistic beauty of its lines. It was a saddle with silver overlays and upholstery which resembled leopard skin. It was crated in a glass covered box to protect it from dampness and be readily available for inspection. It became Juan's job to watch for moisture and mold. As a ranch hand in Argentina, where expensive saddles were used by owners of large ranches, he was familiar with leather maintenance and care.

Early in the morning two days before the New Year, Captain Murphy came down to the chow hall for breakfast and announced, "Men, I have decided to get underway tomorrow morning. There has been a big storm up river. We will have a good flood tide ebbing and the rush of water from the storm, should give us a good push out to sea. I know many of you had your hearts set on staying in port over New Year's Eve. I think we must take advantage of the push toward home."

There was a little soft grumbling from some of the crew. Rosco Quinn said, "I'm getting off in Recife if I can find myself a replacement. I'm not interested in going across the pond again to see Portugal and England. I want to find a ship for New England. It will be nice at home, when I get there, if I go straight up the coast.

The ship left port on the Captain's schedule. She cast off the dock just before daylight and swung around into the river current, heading down stream in a slight fog and mist. Within minutes she was moving at a noticeable rate away from Buenos Aires down the Rio de la Plata toward the open sea. With a good breeze she will clear the mouth of the river and head Northeast before morning on the first day of the New Year.

Mac, being the good steward in providing for the men, had purchased five bottles of wine to celebrate the New Year 1808. Before the midnight hour arrived, the crew members gathered in the chow hall where they sang songs and told stories. Andy was surprised no one was over indulging in the wine. He had always heard sailors were heavy drinkers. He asked Mac why none of the crew drank very much wine and learned it was cooking wine. "I bought cooking wine so there would be some left for me to cook with," he said in reply.

"I should have known you, of all people, would be planning ahead. What do you plan to cook" Andy asked?

"When we were in Rio, I found an English cookbook with wine recipes in it. I believe I will try some of them on the crew for practice. We will have plenty of time after we leave Recife and head for Lisbon. There are several cakes, casseroles and soups with wine I think we can cook."

"You shouldn't say what *we* can cook. I am not a cook and all my experience is cleaning and cutting vegetables. I think wine cooking will be your job," Andy said.

"Oh, I plan to teach you and Juan the art of wine cooking. It will look good on your reports when you go up for officer rank," Mac told him in all seriousness.

At a later date Andy and Juan figured out why Mac wanted them to learn the art of wine cooking. Several times he made something with a strong wine flavor, blaming the boys for not using the right amount. They realized they were his scapegoats, covering his mistakes as he practiced the culinary art of wine cooking.

Heading north again to Recife, the ship was moving slowly, if at all. There was one three day period she moved only fifteen miles, not with the wind, but with ocean currents at the beginning of the Amazon delta. Her navigational log book said she had gone from Recife to Rio in two weeks. The return trip from Rio to Recife took five and a half weeks, much of it becalmed or nearly becalmed.

It was during this period Andy made a discovery while resting on the number two hatch cover watching the sails. He noticed skysails, topsails and royals, the small sails at the top of the masts, would catch a slight breeze and billow forward. At the same time the gallants and mainsails would act as if they were trying to push the ship backward. After watching this happen many times, he found Silas, brought him to the hatch cover and had him watch the sails. He told Silas, "I think the smaller sails are getting a little movement out of the ship in a forward direction. The larger sails, because there is no wind down here, are being backed by the stagnant air at the surface. If we took in the gallants and mainsails, the small sails may move the ship along with the air movement at the upper level."

"I think you might have an idea worth discussing with the Captain. Let's see if he can talk to us now."

They went down to his cabin and he made them wait a couple of minutes as he finished a consignment form. When he was told about Andy's idea he called Lt. Brown from the Navigation office and Andy went over it again for him. Lt. Brown hadn't thought about it but Captain Murphy said he noticed the same action with sails on another ship. After a good discussion, Captain Murphy told Silas to have the crew take in the main sails and see what happens. "If taking in the mains does any good, we'll take in the gallants, too."

Just before sundown the gallants were taken in. By morning it proved the ship had covered at least twelve more miles overnight than previous nights on this northward journey. Andy was happy he had found something to help his uncle Fred Murphy sail faster. "That was good reasoning, Andy," Captain Murphy told him. "Now we will have to find out if your theory holds true under similar conditions."

As the JAVA Sea Sailed into Recife harbor, the lookout saw an available dock, ahead on the right where a small finger of land jutted into the main harbor. He called the information down to the main deck and the ship was turned to head for it as an available docking point. All sails were taken in and the ship secured to the dock. As the crew readied for their noon meal, a man in uniform came aboard and asked why they had tied up at a government dock? When told they were here to pick up cargo consigned for Europe and the United States, they were informed cargo pick ups are now across the harbor. Eating what they could, as fast as they could, the crew went back to work, resetting the rigging to sail one mile across the harbor. This caused some grumbling from the crew, because of the ruined lunch, and the fact, the government man would not allow the cargo to be brought around the harbor on wagons, and loaded at the dock where they were tied up. Captain Murphy promised the Brazilian government and the US consulate were both going to get letters complaining about this incident. "They could have a sign on the dock, indicating only Government Vessels to tie up, and their agent could have come aboard before we were completely secured, to notify us of any restrictions against docking."

For the next two days the crew worked hard loading the number two hold with bags of gold bearing ore. It was headed for refining in the United States, with a consignment to the port at Boston, Massachusetts. Three hundred tons of the ore was placed in the bottom of the hold. Fancy lumber from the Amazon basin completed the load for number two hold. Tomorrow would be February 16, 1808. The Java Sea would leave Brazil behind and head across the Atlantic to Lisbon, Portugal. It would be a long journey with many days at sea doing routine maintenance, standing watches and subconsciously praying they would not become victims of one of those 'perils of the sea,' so commonly referred to in literature.

Captain Murphy called Lt. Brown and Andy to his office to tell them what course he wanted to take to Portugal. "I think we should go northeast from Recife, pick up the thirtieth longitude and head north until we reach the latitude of ten degrees north, there we will make a course correction toward Lisbon, Portugal. Do you think that is a good route northeast, and still clear the African coastline, without getting into areas where Barbary Pirates operate?"

LT. Brown replied, "It sounds like a good route to me."

"I'll just have to agree, because I don't know enough about the subject to have an opinion," Andy told them.

"That's a good answer Andy, I'd hate to be misled if you guessed at something you didn't know," Captain Murphy told him.

CHAPTER 23

▼

The main entry in the log of the Java Sea for February 17, 1808 noted: Sailed from port of Recife, Brazil at 1pm today, heading northeast for 30th longitude. Sailing before a light breeze with main and gallant sails furled, weather clear. Helmsman on duty is John Simmons. Ship's speed is approximately two and one half knots per hour. Apprentice seaman-Cabin boy Murphy reports present position as 32 degrees west and 8 degrees south. Equipment check by Bo's'n Silas Block shows all running gear working as expected.

For the next fourteen days the Java Sea worked its way north, crossing over the equator early on a Tuesday morning while only the watch standers were awake. Later that same day they picked up their first real wind and lowered the gallants and main sails which gradually picked up enough air to billow as a sail should. All was working fine as the Java Sea came out of an area noted for doldrums and becalmed ships. As the ship picked up speed and rolled with the seas under her, even the crew felt happier. Someone started humming a tune. Someone else sang out with an old chantey. The mood and the actions of the crew changed with the change in the ship's movements.

Andy mentioned it to Mac and was told, "Sailors are a happy lot when they're sailing. They get glum when they are just bobbing along over slow rolling waves. It's just their way of life. Their moods fit the mood of the ship."

"It's good to see everyone come to life again," Andy remarked.

"Yes and it is good to see you back to your old self again after your struggle to shake the tropical fever and regain the weight you lost. How are you feeling when everything is considered?" Silas asked him.

"I feel good. I don't think I have any after effects from the fever."

"In that case, how would you like to go up in the crow's nest and relieve the lookout for lunch today?"

"I'd like that. What time should I go up?"

Silas chuckled and said, "That's a silly question, sailor. It makes sense to go up at lunch time. You should eat early lunch and go relieve the lookout for his lunch. I thought you knew the routine of relieving the watch at noontime."

"I've never before relieved the watch at noontime. I was always working in the galley with Mac. Now that Juan has taken over most of the cabin boy duties, I can relieve watches at noon."

"Good, I'll remember that."

When Andy climbed the mast to relieve the watch, he was not surprised to find Willie Wispor in the crow's nest. They greeted each other and after scanning the horizon, Willie left for lunch.

With more exposure to the breeze, it was a few degrees cooler in the crow's nest. It had been hot and stuffy on the main deck most of the time, with only an occasional cooling blast from the steady breeze the Java Sea was dependent on to move her along her chosen course. Andy scanned the horizon every 15 minutes and watched a nearby pod of whales as they swam off the port side of the ship. They too, were headed northeast. The difference between the ship and the whales was the speed. The whales were faster. The ship would need a much stronger breeze to keep abreast of them.

Andy became so enchanted in watching the whales and their maneuvers he forgot to scan the horizon. He was enjoying the sights of giant whales coming halfway out of water, sliding back down, going into a dive with their large tails fanned out behind, before it too slipped out of sight, making hardly a ripple on the surface.

As Andy got back to his duties, he discovered there was a sloop, followed by a brigantine about to come over the eastern horizon. He yelled, "Sail Ho," and answered the helmsman with, "Ten degrees off the starboard bow."

Captain Murphy was notified and he came on deck to look the situation over before deciding to slow down and see what might happen. The sloop crossed over to the port side, turned and fired a shot across the Java Sea's bow as a signal to stop. Captain Murphy told Silas to arm the crew as the two ships drew closer. Coming within hailing distance, the captain of the larger of the two vessels spoke through a megaphone. He said, "Thank you for stopping. I am interested in the sail you were seen flying in front of your vessel. It was orange in color."

Noticing the two ships were gun ships, Captain Murphy asked, "What is your registry?"

The reply came back, "His Majesty's Navy, sailing from Gibraltar. What is your registry?"

"The cargo ship Java Sea, sailing from Baltimore, Maryland, United States registry."

"Well, Yank, can you enlighten us on your orange sail?"

"It is a large triangular sail made of silk. I purchased it in Rio last month from the captain of a Chinese Junk tied up in port there. I had seen him come into port with it flying and it seemed to be working well. I decided it was worth the expense to try it. In this cargo trade speed makes a big difference when moving cargo. We flew it a few times. The drawback is the wind you need for it to be effective. It only works well with a stiff, following wind. A wind more than ten degrees off your heading is not that much help for speed. It also collapses in gusty wind conditions. I'm not sure I can recommend it until I have more experience with it."

"Thank you Captain. That is a good report. I understand what you are saying. Sailing is difficult enough without trying to do it with sails that are not continually dependable. You may proceed. His Majesty's Navy thanks you for your cooperation."

Under his breath Captain Murphy mumbled something to the effect of, "With all those guns pointed at us, what else could I do?"

The ship was brought back to her original course and her speed was gained back in another hour. Lisbon was still many miles away. They were now at latitude 20 degrees North and longitude 30 degrees. Day and night they sailed on with the routine becoming ever more boring. Nothing of interest had happened since the whales and the British Navy encounter. The crew was getting edgy and a couple of guys got into a fist fight over a stale piece of toast.

Silas kept them apart by placing them on different watches and working one forward and the other aft. Three days later one of them came to Silas and said he wanted to apologize to the other man. The apology was accepted and the two became friends again as if nothing had gone awry between them.

For weeks the ship plowed along without ever making a good run in a twenty-four hour period. All the old timers knew they were sailing in an area often devoid of strong, steady wind. One day they hit two squalls with strong winds that lasted a half hour or more. The second squall had quite a large amount of hail in it. The crew caught all they could to add to their water for a refreshing drink. This proved a rare treat and was discussed often for a few days. Old hands told stories of hail squalls at sea, some of long duration, others with hail as large as apples. They told of hail squalls tearing the sails and rigging off a ship. Both boys, Andy and Juan were impressed with many of the stories being told.

Another time a flock of birds the size of small ducks landed in the rigging and on the yardarms. They rode along for an hour or more, apparently resting their wings, then left heading in a southeasterly direction. Speculation among the crew was the birds were flying from Europe to Africa and had flown off course to be this far west of their usual routes. Because of this unusual happening with the birds, Lt. Brown decided he should do a calibration on the sextant to make sure it had not become out of adjustment.

The sextant proved to be out of adjustment and once it was corrected they discovered they were more than one hundred fifty miles northeast of the point they were at the noon reading. As serious as it was, the two boys joked about traveling one hundred fifty miles in one hour. That's a speed record for this old ship they laughed.

The following morning Andy had the crows nest watch from 8 until noon. About an hour into the watch he thought he saw a small sail like a skysail on the horizon but it never got any larger and finally went back down out of sight astern of the Java Sea. He mentioned it to Silas and he said, "It was probably a Portuguese fisherman. They fish these waters on a regular basis."

The next day, the ship was surrounded by Portuguese fishermen in their small boats. Mac hailed them and finally got one of them to understand he wanted to buy some fish. The deal was made with a lot of hand signaling and jibber jabbering no one really understood. The end result was a good fish dinner for the crew.

Three weeks later the Java Sea docked in Lisbon on a Saturday morning. She unloaded fourteen mahogany logs that afternoon and was told the dock crew would return on Monday. Saturday evening the crew went ashore and watched the local people celebrate a religious festival in preparation for Sunday church services. There was singing, dancing and tables of food on several of the main streets. The crew was invited to participate with the locals as they celebrated. Andy and Juan helped themselves to some of the food on one of the tables. When they were finished eating, two young girls came to them to dance. They tried to explain they could not dance but the girls, talking in Portuguese which Juan partially understood, said because the boys had eaten the food the girls had prepared they would have to dance with them until the festival ended at midnight. A glance at the local people standing around watching over the girls, told the boys they better learn to dance and learn fast. By midnight all four of the young people were having a good time together and made plans to go for a walk to see the town, once the girls were out of church on Sunday afternoon.

They walked up one street and down another. They went to a small museum and toured an old building. They had a fancy cookie as a treat from a local bakery. For supper, in a small restaurant, not far from the center of town, where they had danced the day before, they had something similar to a sandwich made in a Portuguese roll. It was delicious. When the boys asked the girls what kind of meats were in the sandwich, the best answer they could get was, "Guess."

They found the girls names were Bragaretta and Moriea. As they left the restaurant the sun was beginning to go down behind the taller trees. The girls indicated they had to go home. It was a four block walk to Bragaretta's and one more block to Moriea's. As they walked, Moriea reached for Andy's hand and told Juan to tell him she enjoyed his dancing and visiting with her. As they went up the four or five steps to Moriea's front door, she stopped and told him to come with her around the corner of the house. There, in the shadows, she gave him a big kiss, right on his lips. It was his first kiss from a girl in a romantic way. He wasn't quite sure what to do to respond other than kiss back, which he did. He gave her a big hug with his arms completely wrapped around her. Looking her straight in the eye, he said, "I am sorry I have to go. That was my first kiss from a girl. Thank you."

He was taken aback when Moriea said in English, with a slight Portuguese accent, "I thought it might be. You and Juan act like a couple of boys who are on their first job away from home. Am I right?"

"Yes, we are cabin boys and I am in training to be a navigator. Why didn't you tell me you spoke English?"

"I wanted to test you to find out what kind of person you would be when you found out. It was more interesting to hear you and Juan try to figure out what to say to us. Bragaretta doesn't speak English. We had a good time with you."

She gave him another small kiss, this time on the cheek and said, "Good Night, Andy."

Walking back to meet Juan, Andy thought about what had happened to him in Lisbon. He liked being kissed, but he didn't like being misled, and lied to, by Moriea. He was happy the girls had guided them to so many points of interest. As soon as he got back with Juan, he told him about the ruse Moriea had pulled on them. "I know," Juan replied, "While we were walking to the museum, Bragaretta told me Moriea could speak English. She said I should keep it a secret because Moriea wanted to tell you herself when the time was right."

"I just don't like being lied to," Andy said. "I believed Moriea and was beginning to like her, when she pulled off a big lie to deceive us. It isn't right."

"Don't shout about it. It wasn't our fault."

"I know that. I'm just angry about it."

The following morning the Java Sea finished her unloading and picked up a small load of fish boxes consigned to Nova Scotia. She let go the dock at 2:45 in the afternoon and swung out into the harbor heading for Plymouth, England. Andy was in the crow's nest for the afternoon watch. Standing on the end of the dock were the two girls, Moriea and Bragaretta, waving their handkerchiefs as a goodbye to Andy and Juan. Once Andy saw them, he pulled out his old, red bandana and waved back. In forty minutes, with a good breeze, the Java Sea crossed the harbor and turned through the narrows toward the open sea. In the crow's nest, Andy was still waving his bandana. On the dock, the girls were still waving their frilly, little handkerchiefs.

CHAPTER 24

▼

With a strong breeze the ship soon left Lisbon, Portugal far enough behind it was not possible to distinguish anything but the form of the land. In the late afternoon a Portuguese fisherman came along side and Mac bought some fresh fish, consisting mostly of cod and haddock. There were a couple of sea eels for sale and Mac bought one for his own supper. "Most people won't eat eels," Mac said. "I happen to like them." He told Andy and Juan he would let them taste it when he fried it. Andy was happy to try it. Juan turned it down long before it was cooked.

During the next few days as they sailed northerly toward England, several ships came within hailing distance. The usual questions asked of the Java Sea were; 'How long did it take you from one port to another?' 'Have you had good sailing with strong winds?' 'Did you have any damage from storms?' 'Where are you going next?'

Only one ship passed without hailing or answering a hail from Captain Murphy. It was a large Russian cargo ship under full sail. With only a very small Russian flag flying from her mizzen mast, she was hard to identify. At more than 200 yards distance it was impossible to identify her tiny flag without using a long glass. Most Russian ships were secretive of their movements.

As the ship drew closer to Plymouth, England, Captain Murphy and Lt. Brown studied the charts to learn about entering the harbor. Lt. Brown said, "Rosco Quinn has been in and out of here several times. Should we ask him if he knows anything specific we should be alerted to when entering the docking area?"

"That's a good idea. I'll send for him and we'll ask if he knows anything of importance." With that, Captain Murphy called Juan telling him to find Rosco and have him come to the Navigational Office.

When asked about entering Plymouth, Rosco told them he had been helmsman on several trips in and out of the busy port. He said, "The main key is keeping well to the north side of the channel and swinging in as the point is cleared. It means the sails have to be put on the opposite tack at just the right time to keep from losing headway. The harbor is small for a ship this size and you will need to let go on all sails very quickly. We can do it but it has to be done fast."

"Thank you Rosco. It's always helpful when we have a crew member who knows about ports we are not familiar with. Both Lt. Brown and I have been in and out of here once or twice years ago. We will probably ask you to take the helm when we enter."

The next afternoon Willie Wispor with his sharp eyes manned the crows nest, Rosco Quinn at the helm and Captain Murphy giving orders, the good ship Java Sea sailed into Plymouth, England as if she was the local ferry on a daily run. She made fast to a dock that didn't look solid enough to hold a ship the size of the Java Sea. Once made fast, Captain Murphy and Silas went ashore to contact the consignee for the cargo of lumber and logs destined for Plymouth. While they were gone a gentleman came aboard looking for the Captain. When told the Captain was ashore with no scheduled return time, he asked if he could wait. Lt. Brown told him he would be welcome and could sit at a table in the mess hall, offering him a cup of coffee.

"Thank you," he said. "My name is Commander Cyrus Ogden."

When he came down to the mess hall, Andy and Juan waited on him, providing him with a mug of coffee and sugar as sweetener. He told the boys he was a Commander in the English Naval Service and was being transferred to Nova Scotia. He had been serving on a ship in the North Sea and this was a new assignment. "I'm sure Nova Scotia Canada cannot be as cold and blustery as the North Sea." He also asked where the Java Sea had been and how long the boys had served on her. He showed particular interest in her average speed and if she rode well in rough seas. Having never been on other ships, the boys told him they had nothing to compare her with.

Mac and Lt. Brown came to sit at the table with Commander Ogden and the boys. Andy told the Commander, "Lieutenant Brown and Mac will be able to answer your questions about the speed and motion in rough seas."

Directing his questions again to the Lieutenant and Mac, the Commander listened intently as they talked about the ship.

"I have been aboard for three years and find she handles well in heavy seas. She rides well for a large cargo ship and her speed is in the upper end of the range of sailing ships, mostly due to the competency of our Captain and crew," Lt. Brown told him.

"I have been sailing with Captain Murphy for fourteen years. He is the best I know when it comes to operating a cargo ship. He has considerable compassion for his crew and runs a ship with the crew's safety as the first order of business. We have always had a skillful, happy crew working in a team effort. There have been few instances of friction during my fourteen years with captain Murphy. This is the third ship he has commanded, each one larger than the previous."

Captain Murphy and Silas came back aboard and were introduced to Commander Ogden. The Captain excused himself while he told Silas to prepare the ship for unloading the logs and lumber in the morning. "I don't want to depend on the lumber people being on time. We can off load using the mizzen and foremast while we are waiting for them to get here. I think there is enough time before dark to get the ship prepared."

Once Commander Ogden finished his introduction to the Captain they discussed his need for passage to Nova Scotia for himself and his family consisting of a wife and two children, a daughter fourteen and a son age nine. Captain Murphy told him the Java Sea was not prepared to carry passengers and was strictly a cargo ship. The Commander pleaded, offering to pay double the normal fare to get his family to America on a sailing with himself. He told Captain Murphy he was being transferred to a Naval Coastal Command station outside Halifax and must get there as soon as possible. He said he could not find another ship going to Nova Scotia. In order to accommodate the Commander, Captain Murphy agreed to move the Navigation Office into the hold where the lumber would be removed.

"I am doing this to assist you with your transportation problem," the Captain told him. "Ordinarily I would refuse to take passengers. You and your family must adhere to strict seagoing safety and instructions of the crew. The children will wear lifejackets at all times when top side and never climb on any rigging."

"Captain Murphy, as a seagoing man I am aware of your concerns and will assure you we will keep a close eye on our children during this passage. I believe they are well trained and will not cause problems. They also know I am a strict disciplinarian," Commander Ogden said.

"Where are you staying in Plymouth?" Captain Murphy asked.

"We are renting an apartment on a weekly basis. It is paid until the end of next week. We can get a refund for unused days."

"In that event I believe you had best come aboard tomorrow afternoon about one o'clock. I hope to sail the following morning with the ebb tide. I have been given to understand there is a good chance of an offshore breeze during early morning hours. It would be nice to clear the harbor into the open ocean soon after breakfast," Captain Murphy said.

"We will see you next about one o'clock tomorrow afternoon. Thank You Captain. I am sure we will enjoy sailing on your vessel. I hope you will enjoy having us as your passengers."

Before Commander Ogden was off the ship, Captain Murphy called Lt. Brown and Silas to tell them about moving the charts and making a bedroom for the Ogdens out of the Navigation office.

Mac aroused Andy and Juan at 4:30 the next morning to assist him with breakfast and the usual coffee run to the officers. They rushed through the quick and easy to do chores before beginning to cook sausage, pancakes and scrambled eggs. Juan made the coffee run to the officers while Mac prepared the pancake batter. Andy was cracking eggs into a large container from which they would be ladled to the grill. Once everything was nearly ready Andy went to wake Silas and the crew, dropping off a cup of coffee to the night gangway watch.

John Simmons had the watch and was happy to get the coffee. He asked Andy, "How have you been feeling lately?

"I think I am completely cured. I feel like my weight is back to normal, my breathing is easier and I don't get tired as often as I did two weeks ago. I sure owe everyone, especially you, a bunch of thank you speeches for all the care I received."

"Well kid, I'm glad you are doing better now. I was worried about after effects," John told him.

The crew was still eating breakfast when four gigantic wagons, each pulled by two matched pairs of large draft horses, came onto the dock. Each team of four was Belgians, Clydesdales or crossbreeds. They were an impressive sight on the dock at six o'clock in the morning. Behind them was another gigantic wagon pulled by four oxen. That wagon was built to hold stacks of logs and could be tipped to roll the logs off. At the same time, coming up the gangway was a stout little man with a thin moustache and bushy sideburns. He wore a derby hat, short jacket, with a Macdonald Clan kilt hanging above Argyle knee-length sox protruding out of his logging boots.

He introduced himself to the gangway watchman and asked to speak to the Captain. John Simmons led him down to the Captain's cabin and after introductions returned to his watch.

Angus Macdonald paid Captain Murphy a pre offload fee with the rest promised at the conclusion of the work. He told Captain Murphy he would like to load the ox drawn wagon first because oxen are not as patient as horses when standing around waiting to be loaded. "We can load both wagons at the same time by using the foremast and mizzen as our loading points. If you pull your ox team to the area near the gangway, we can give you two logs or more with every lift. The lumber from the after hold was set on the dock yesterday afternoon. We can pick it up from there and load you after the oxen and logs have moved out of the way."

"It sounds like you have the job already started and planned in an efficient manner," Angus said.

"We are fortunate on this ship to have one of the most dedicated Boatswain Mates of any ship I have knowledge of sailing in the Atlantic cargo trade. He has been with me for fourteen years and is a dependable man. He is very capable when it comes to the ship's operations and motivation of the crew," Captain Murphy informed Angus.

Time passed rapidly during the off loading. Andy managed a few minutes to go ashore to be close to the draft horses and oxen. He asked one of the drovers if he could pat one of the horses and was told it would be alright if his hands were clean. Not understanding the remark, he looked quizzically to the drover. The old man smiled and gave him a wink before asking, "Have you been around horses before, lad?"

"I grew up on a Maryland farm in the United States," he replied. "We had a pair of Clydesdales to do the farm work. They were good gentle animals."

"I have been around this type of horse for over fifty years, as a drover for the last forty, I've not seen any ill tempered ones," the old drover said.

"Thank you, sir. I must get back to my job," Andy told him, walking past the oxen to give one a pat on his fore shoulder.

The lumber and logs were on the dock well before noon. The third lumber wagon left the dock at 11:25, leaving the fourth wagon to complete the work. The ox drawn load of logs had pulled away before eight o'clock. Three bundles of boards were set on the fourth wagon, two end to end and one on top. A fast tie down by the drover finished the work on the dock.

The crew stopped for the noon meal leaving all the lines used in off loading lying around the deck, hanging from the masts and yardarms in a general upheaval.

Commander Ogden and his family arrived while the crew was eating. Their driver set their baggage at the end of the gangway. They made their way up to the main deck and seeing no one, Commander Ogden went down below looking for Captain Murphy. Not finding him aft, he went forward and found him in the chow hall. Surprised to see him so much earlier than the appointed boarding time, Captain Murphy was slightly angered. Controlling himself he said, "If you have your family with you we should bring them down to the chow hall and give them some lunch, it will be a few minutes before we have the decks cleared enough to move you into your berthing space."

Andy and Juan went up to the main deck to assist the family safely to the chow hall. While young Samuel Ogden made his own way over all the ropes and gear lying around, Juan helped Elizabeth Ogden with Andy's instruction. Andy helped Rebecca. He later told Juan his instinct warned him to help Rebecca. "She looked like a girl who would need his greater experience to guide her around the ship," he reasoned.

Introductions were made by Captain Murphy to those crew members present. "Although transporting passengers is something new for the Java Sea, I trust all crew members will make their trip as comfortable and pleasant as possible. It is mandatory the children wear life preservers at all times on the weather decks. It is absolutely not permissible for passengers to climb on the rigging. Work is being done on the ship at all times. The Ogdens and their children should be welcome observers as long as they watch from a safe distance."

Turning to the table where the Ogdens were seated he told the parents it would be their responsibility to oversee the children's deportment. "As a Commander in the Royal Navy, you understand the necessity of keeping a tight rein on youngsters aboard a ship this size. I'm sure you have instructed them in good behavior during this passage."

"Our children are home schooled because of the many moves we make while I am in His Majesty's service. I feel confident they will not present a problem. I also expect your crew to guide them in their wanderings, keeping them out of areas where they should not explore."

"Thank you Commander. As for your comfort, Mrs. Ogden, I will have Silas rig a hammock on the southerly side of the wheelhouse, where you will be able to sit on the few warm, sunny days we will encounter on a North Atlantic crossing. I am also sure Mac will always welcome your input in the galley. I imagine you could give him some tips on spices and cooking times. I'll close saying, we all welcome you on our ship."

Elizabeth spoke with a lady like high pitched voice as she said, "Thank you, Captain Murphy. I am sure we will enjoy sailing with you and your crew."

Silas, speaking to the crew said, "We will let go the dock at 5 o'clock in the morning. Lieutenant Brown will take the helm. The high men will let go the Sky, Royal and Topsails. Once we clear the harbor and head into the open sea, we will set the Gallants and Main Sheets. After breakfast we should be nearing the point of land known as Land's End. Once we clear it, if all is running well, we will set the studding sail and head for the American side of the Atlantic."

A rousing cheer went up from the crew. There were a lot of back slaps, hand shakes and loud whistles as the men danced around the chow hall, happy to be going in a direction that would eventually take them home. Like every sailor before them, going home after two years at sea, was the answer to their dreams.

The afternoon was spent clearing the deck of all the ropes and pulleys used to unload the lumber. Andy and Juan assisted the Ogdens with their baggage and looking in various storage places to find extra things they needed. John Simmons and a new man named Arthur Reid, hoisted their trunks aboard using the lines from the lumber work, still attached to the mizzen mast. Three trunks and four suitcases were set on the poop deck for easy transfer into their room. The two cabin boys carried everything to the room.

About 4:30 that afternoon the Java Sea was back in her usual state of readiness for sea. Andy and Juan were both helping Mac with evening meal preparations. Rebecca and Samuel came into the chow hall and asked if they could watch what they do to get ready to serve a meal. "All the action is here in the galley," Mac yelled to her. "You won't learn anything watching the cabin boys, it's the cook who does it all." He followed it with one of his big chuckles, knowing he was teasing Juan and Andy.

CHAPTER 25

▼

The early morning crew was up before 4 o'clock, most of them sitting in the chow hall drinking a cup of coffee for an eye opener. Mac, being a kind and considerate man beneath his unpolished, rough exterior brought out some hastily made rolls with cinnamon and sugar filling. "This will have to hold you together until we get underway and I can feed you a regular breakfast," he said.

Although he had always had coffee ready under like circumstances, this was the first time he had made cinnamon rolls to go with his early morning pick-me-up.

William Isley spoke up. "This is real nice of you Mac. We know you're a good cook and have our best interests at heart. I hope you keep up these surprises. We also know your job isn't the easiest one with meals and the business end of the galley on your shoulders. I think we all believe you deserve more than you get for the job you do."

Silas walked in, returned his coffee mug to the tray and said, "Men the sky is beginning to lighten, the tide has already turned. It is time we let go and set sail. Let's go home."

The ship was free of the dock before five o'clock. All upper sails were set as she moved across the harbor toward an opening which would take her to the open sea. A good tide was running, helping her gain speed. She eased through the passage and picked up a slightly stronger breeze, filling the upper sails, keeping them taught. Land's End was fifteen miles west. There the English Channel would open into the Atlantic Ocean, leaving only open sea to Nova Scotia.

Once clear of the harbor the crew went to breakfast. After they had eaten they checked out the rigging lines for the gallants and main sails on all three masts.

Willie Wispor found a frayed down haul on the forward main sail. A new one was run through the blocks and made fast to a belaying pin with other foremast lines. The good parts of the frayed rope were cut into pieces for making repair and emergency splices.

At nine o'clock, Andy took the morning position reading and as he was checking the sextant, he saw some movement out of the corner of his left eye. He turned to find Rebecca standing on the poop deck watching him. He said, "Good morning."

She said, "Good morning," and asked, "What are you doing?"

"I am taking a reading on the sun to figure the ship's position. We do it two times a day. Would you like to watch and learn how we do it?"

"Will it be alright? I don't want to be in the way."

"You won't be in the way. Come on down and I'll show you how the sextant works. We will then go down to the navigational office and figure out where we were at the moment I took the reading."

From that morning on, Rebecca was a tag along to Andy when he was doing navigation readings. She was not familiar with math and could not grasp the way to solve the problem. Triangulation was a word she had never heard before. She told Andy he was smart and she liked that in a man. She took an interest in his chores and often helped him in the chow hall to set or clean tables. He liked her company. Two days she helped him repair sails in the sail locker. She enjoyed being with him.

Often, when he was on watch in the crows nest, he would look down and she would be sitting on the deck, leaning against the wheel house, looking up to where he was standing in the lookout barrel. He would wave to her and she would wave back with a big smile on her face. Thus, the two became good friends on the way to Nova Scotia. The trip lasted seventeen days. They were blown back in one storm, losing at least a full day of sailing time. It was the worst storm they had encountered in their time at sea. Old timers said things like that were expected in the North Atlantic.

Commander Ogden spent much of his time with Captain Murphy and Lt. Brown. Elizabeth Ogden spent most of the fair weather days in the hammock on the side of the wheelhouse. Little Samuel Ogden was the favorite of the crew. Every man aboard, at one time or another, spent time teaching him knots, painting, woodworking and even scrimshaw on an old piece of soup bone. The crew enjoyed the passengers and the passengers enjoyed the crew.

Both of the Ogden children were excited when they told their parents what they were doing or learning from the crew members as they worked on most of the ship's routine duties. Where Samuel was busy helping all of the crew, Rebecca almost always prefaced her remarks with, "Andy taught me" or, "I helped Andy." His name was always a part of her discussions with Commander and Elizabeth Ogden.

The Andy, Rebecca relationship was not all one sided. Andy looked up from figuring the ship's position one morning and said, "I like having you helping me with my duties. It makes my work seem more important."

"I'm pleased you like having me help you because I love being around you and watching how you do your jobs on the ship. I think you are a special young man. I like being near you."

They were in the midst of taking the late afternoon sextant readings when the lookout shouted "Land Ho, ten degrees off the starboard bow."

Both Andy and Rebecca looked in the direction indicated but could see nothing. "That's Willie up there. He has extremely sharp vision. He has a long glass and most likely the land is below the horizon to us on the deck."

Two hours later there was a lot of land to be seen off to starboard. It was identified as Morris Point at the entrance to Halifax Harbor. Daylight was fast ending. Captain Murphy decided to anchor off the point until morning before attempting to enter a strange harbor late in the day, knowing it would be dark before they could tie up to a dock. He sent Silas and Lt. Brown in a small boat to contact the harbor master for a berth and find out where the ship could be careened. Commander Ogden went with them to seek information about his new assignment in Nova Scotia.

Once the ship was anchored and the night meal was over, the dishes cleaned and put away, Andy and Rebecca stood by the rail on the poop deck looking out over the land. They could see several buildings with lights in them and talked about what they imagined could be happening in different shaped buildings. One small building down near the point caught their eye and they decided it was the home of a young man and wife with two small children, a boy and a girl. They continued, talking about what it would be like to have a home and family of their own. "Will you still go to sea after you get married and have your own family?" Rebecca asked.

"I don't think so. I have decided I would like to stay ashore and get a degree in engineering from the college in Baltimore. If I buy a nice riding horse I can stay at home and ride to and from school each day. Five days a week with all the vacation times considered wouldn't be too hard on either me or the horse. It would be a five mile ride each way. I have to talk to my parents when I get home to make sure it will be OK with them for me to stay home and go to school."

"Oh, that's a good idea Andy. I think you'd be wise to follow that plan. I also want you to know I have enjoyed these past seventeen days coming to Halifax on your ship. Being with you, I have learned to love you. I have made up my mind to leave home when I am eighteen, find you and we can get married."

Andy stood dumbfounded at what she had said. He liked her and she was a nice looking, clean cut girl, but marriage with him turning fourteen next month. He stood frozen in his tracks. She turned to him, threw her arms up over his shoulders and kissed him solidly on his lips. He put his arms up and reached around her, hugging her close, giving her a good friendly kiss in return. It was time to say good night. Tomorrow they would head up the harbor to unload the Portuguese fish boxes and leave the Ogdens in Halifax.

The anchor was raised and the Java Sea headed up the channel toward Halifax Harbor. Captain Murphy called a conference with Commander Ogden, Lt. Brown and Silas. He told them he thought the best approach would be to stay close to McNab Island on the way in. After clearing McNab, they would make a hard turn to port heading for Point Pleasant. About 100 feet from the Point they would drop the starboard anchor and let the ship swing around it, dropping the port anchor when the ship was aligned to back into the harbor. The anchors could then be used to align the ship with the docks, letting off line as needed to warp the ship into the dock at the foot of Inglis Street. A look at the harbor chart indicated the Captain was going to pull off a slick maneuver to save time and prevent having to go to Bedford Basin, turn around and come back to the dock.

Silas said, "That's a tough maneuver. I think our crew is up to doing it. The timing will have to be near perfect. We'll need close oversight from you to do it, Captain."

"We will have Lt. Brown on the fo'c'sle. I will be in the wheelhouse and on the poop deck. Commander Ogden has offered to watch from the crows nest for obstacles and any ships with the right of way. Silas will be watching and overseeing the crew." After a slight pause Captain Murphy asked, "What do you say gentlemen, shall we try it?"

They all agreed there was good reason to try it and if anyone could do it, this crew was the crew who could.

Two hours later the ship was tied to the dock. Nearly a parade of old time sailors came to tell the crew they had never seen such a maneuver in Halifax Harbor before. They were all praise for the seamanship demonstrated. One old sailor said, "I'm aged ninety-three and I spent most of my life at sea. Never before have I seen such beautiful handling of a large ship. I thank you for the demonstration of your skills as seamen."

Number one and three hatches were opened and the fish boxes were partially unloaded. The pile became so big on the dock there was no room left to lower any more boxes. Again they were confronted with the lack of workers on a weekend to move the cargo away as they placed it on the dock.

Captain Murphy walked along the dock talking to the old timers about a place in the Bay of Fundy to careen the ship to repair a couple of planks located below the waterline. He was referred to Jeb Snow who told him the best place for a ship the size of the Java Sea was on a thin finger of land with a few fishermen's shanties called Digby Neck. Go up that reach with the Neck on your port side. You'll find plenty of places to lay her over in there. "Digby Neck is on the Nova Scotia side at the mouth of the bay. You'd best go about five to ten miles in from the deep water," Jeb told him.

Captain Murphy thanked him and started to walk back toward the ship. An elderly man and lady pulled up in a carriage beside him and asked, "Are you the Captain of that big ship ahead there?"

"Yes," he replied.

"I heard about your tricky entrance to our harbor. Any man who can sail that size vessel and back into a dock is a man after my own heart. I am retired Commodore Whitney, this is my wife Anabelle. Could I walk her around your main deck to show her what a real sailor's ship looks like when it is tied to the dock?"

"I am Captain Murphy. It will be a pleasure to have you aboard. If you would like I will walk around the deck with you to answer any questions the lady might have. There may be several new changes in cargo ships since your sailing days, Commodore."

Mrs. Whitney spoke, "That will be very generous of you Captain Murphy. Do you have a family somewhere?"

"Yes, I have a wife, a daughter ten and a five year old son in Baltimore, Maryland. We have been away from the home port for nearly two years now. The crew and I are anxious to get home again. I expect we will be there in another month and a half, if we have good winds going down the coast."

While they were talking they had been walking around the decks and Commodore Whitney explained some of the running lines to his wife. A few of the crew were busy doing some maintenance. Captain Murphy introduced them to crew members working on the main deck. Mac offered them a cup of coffee or tea which was declined.

When the Commodore broached the subject of the ship's entrance into the harbor, as they were standing at the head of the gangway before leaving, Captain Murphy said, "I have a special crew aboard this ship. Most have been with me for over ten years. They are all skilled in their jobs. This ship is blessed to have the crew it has, doing the jobs they do. I will give credit to each one, but my bo's'n is the most skilled sailor I have had the pleasure of knowing in my seventeen years at sea."

"It's been a thrill to come aboard such a fine working cargo vessel and meet several of you. I thank you for the tour. It isn't often a woman gets to do such things. Although the Commodore has gone ahead to get the carriage, I am sure you brought back pleasant memories to him today. If you ever lay over in Halifax again, we live on Pleasant Drive, please come and have supper with us, Charles would love it and so would I."

"Thank you Mrs. Whitney, I'll keep that in my mind. Good Bye."

"Good Bye, Captain Murphy." She turned and walked down the gangway.

CHAPTER 26

▼

Unloading was completed the next day. Captain Murphy decided to remain tied to the dock and leave a day later. After the evening meal, Commodore Ogden decided to take his family for a walk along the row of docks on the waterfront. Rebecca asked Andy to walk with her behind the parents. Without much pleading he agreed to come along. The five of them strolled along in a relaxed manner, the parents and Samuel about a city block ahead of Andy and Rebecca.

Suddenly from between two buildings a pair of local ruffians jumped out and tried to abduct Rebecca. The echo of her scream had not ended when Andy pulled a belaying pin from the top of his right boot and cracked the closest boy across the shin. He came up swinging the belaying pin into the second boy's arm. Before they had a chance to recover from the first blows, boy number one received a sharp blow to the side of his head which bounced off striking the second boy across the forehead. Andy bent and smacked the kneecaps of each boy, causing them to fall to their knees and roll over on their sides in pain. He stepped back to check the condition of Rebecca just as her father arrived to assist in the battle.

The two boys managed to get to their feet and limped off crying with painful head aches and especially sore kneecaps. Andy watched them go back between the two buildings from which they had come. He believed he had left enough marks they wouldn't come back for more. Rebecca was still whimpering from fright when she came over to him and threw her arms around him, called him her hero and kissed him soundly while her parents watched.

The Commodore took his hand and gave it a good, firm shake. He asked, "Where did you learn the art of defense with a belaying pin? You certainly earned my indebtedness by saving my daughter. I think you earned hers too."

"The crew schooled me on belaying pin defense and Mac told me I should always carry one when I was walking around the docks on evenings. We are fortunate the new Halifax gas lights are working. It's easier to protect yourself when you can see."

As they were walking back to the ship a messenger rode up on a horse and asked if we had a Commodore Ogden aboard. "I'm Commodore Ogden. My family and I were taking a stroll along the dock and are now on our way to the ship. May I help you?"

"Yes sir, I have a sealed message for you and will need to see some form of identification before I can turn it over. It is from the Admiralty and has been in our office for over a month, waiting for you to appear."

"Where is the Admiralty Office located?" he asked. "I could not locate it yesterday when I was looking for it at the Oxford Street Address on my orders."

"There is no Admiralty Office in Halifax now. They reduced its size and moved it to Montreal," the messenger replied.

Commodore Ogden produced sufficient identification and received the message in a sealed pouch. He carried it aboard where he and his wife went to their room to open it. Much to his surprise, he had been transferred to Washington, DC as a Naval Attache to the British Embassy. He immediately made arrangements with Captain Murphy to continue on to Baltimore.

As planned the ship got underway with the outgoing tide the next morning. It was a nice smooth cruise along the coast of Nova Scotia to the mouth of the Bay of Fundy. Captain Murphy sailed into the Bay and found the finger of land he had been told about. He climbed up beside the lookout and used his long glass to study the shore of Digby Neck. Picking a spot between Little River and East Ferry, a long Boat was readied. The Captain and Silas went ashore to check for the best beaching place. Willie Wispor and Ed Smith went as rowers. The Commodore went as an observer.

During the day and a half they had sailed from Halifax, the crew was busy tying everything down and loading much of it against the starboard side where it would not upset as the ship was laid on her starboard side. The following day the ship waited until the tide started out to make her run for the shore. She grounded and nearly everyone lost their balance as she came to a sudden stop.

Tides went out fast in the Bay of Fundy and it was only a short time before the Java Sea started to lie over to starboard. As soon as the bad planks cleared the water, William Isley, with a box of carpenter tools, was lowered over the side on a plank staging. Within a half hour he had the rotten planking torn loose. Silas and Ed Smith were inside the hull, knocking out the pieces as soon as Isley got the caulking seams cleared. Once the ship settled into the sand and there was no more movement, a staging was lowered where two or three men could insert the new planks and spike them into place.

When the tide changed and started coming back into St Mary Bay it ran fast. The bay filled with water coming in layers of tidal bore. The repair had been completed with time to spare. When high tide arrived, the Java Sea floated clear of the sandy beach and with her sails set at an angle she moved out into the narrow bay headed for the open sea once more.

Just before sundown, the ship cleared Brier Island on her starboard side and turned southwesterly to skirt the coast of Maine. She was back in the Atlantic Ocean again with a fair breeze off her starboard quarter. It looked like she would be in for a night of good sailing. Andy was busy with the sextant, shooting the late day sun for a position reading. Rebecca was with him, jabbering about how lucky they were her father was transferred to Washington and they could be together until they got to Baltimore. "I'm glad you're happy," he told her.

"Do you know why you said that?" she asked.

"Said what?" he answered.

"That you are glad I'm happy."

"Oh, I'm glad when anyone is happy. I like happy people."

"Now you said you like me because I'm happy. That's a good start. What I want to hear is you say you love me."

Catching him slightly off guard, he blurted out, "Of course I do."

Lt. Brown walked out of the makeshift Navigation Office and asked Andy if he got a good positioning with the readings he took before sundown.

"I think so. In fact, I'm sure of it. There was very little ship movement to interfere."

"Good, I'll check your figures later. We should be sailing in good open water tonight. I'm getting somewhat hungry. I think I'll go to supper now. Have you folks had your supper?"

"We always eat after the crew is finished, wash dishes, clean the chow hall and start preparations for morning. It is easier to do it at night than get up early to get everything set up. We'll see you later, Sir."

As the ship sailed for home, everything was quiet and peaceful except for an occasional squeal, high on a mast, from a piece of rigging as it shifted in the steady breeze. Andy and Rebecca sat on the top step of the ladder leading to the poop deck, with their feet hanging down over the edge of the steps, talking about their days together and what a nice time they've had since leaving England twenty six days ago. They promised to write each other when they were at a permanent address. Andy took a piece of paper out of his pocket and said, "My home address is on this paper. You can write me there and I'll get it. That's our farm."

The ship was making lazy rolls to port and starboard as they sailed along at an estimated five knots. Rebecca sitting beside Andy would let her head relax and fall with the roll when the ship leaned to port. Her head would end up against Andy's shoulder with her hair brushing his cheek and the side of his face. He noticed it. He didn't complain. He liked it. When she said she was getting chilly, he unbuttoned his jacket, took his arm out of one sleeve, put one of her arms in the empty sleeve and wrapped half of his jacket around her in such a way they were both sharing the jacket.

"You are so sweet and thoughtful of me, it is no wonder I fell in love with you on this voyage."

"You're a victim of the fresh, salt air and a gently rolling Java Sea tonight. You are being influenced by the circumstances you are surrounded with. You'll change your mind by the time you are old enough to get married."

"No. You are the influence. Between England and Halifax, I decided I really cared for you and the feeling deepened as we got acquainted, seeing you every day, working with you and watching you in the crows nest. Then, in Halifax when you saved me from those ruffians, it really caused me to fall deeply in love with you. You are a good man Andy Murphy. I love you and someday I am going to be your wife."

Rebecca's determination to love him and become his wife left him tongue tied. He didn't know what to say. He sat silently, sharing his jacket with her, wondering what the future would hold for them. He knew when they reached Baltimore they would be going separate ways, with perhaps an occasional letter as a future contact.

Six days later the ship made a turn to starboard and headed up the long stretch of Chesapeake Bay. They should be tying up to the Curtis Bay dock in about thirty hours. Andy will be home.

Shadowed by Rebecca much of the final few hours aboard, he busied himself with his usual routine and making farewell contacts with crew members. It was difficult to say good bye to each and every one, but when he got to Silas and Mac, his throat turned hoarse and tears welled in his eyes. He found himself thinking,

'It isn't easy to say good bye to my shipmates, who have been my friends and companions for two years in the close living conditions aboard ship.'

As soon as the Java Sea docked, the crew went to work stripping away the sails, unloading cargo and saying farewells to those leaving early. Baggage and trunks were hoisted ashore for the Ogdens. The bureau and gifts Andy had bought for his mother and sisters were set on the dock and covered with a piece of water-proofing until he could go to the farm and bring back a wagon to carry them home.

A livery wagon came to pick up the Ogdens and their baggage to take them to Baltimore where they could arrange transportation to Washington and the British Embassy. Commodore Ogden sought Andy and found him with Rebecca on the poop deck beside the wheelhouse. He told Rebecca to go with her mother and get in the wagon. She turned first and gave Andy a big kiss, ignoring her father's presence. They both promised to write to each other.

With Rebecca heading down the gangway, Commodore Ogden informed Andy he was aware his daughter had made plans in her head to marry him when she was old enough to become his wife. He said, "Andy, I think you would make a fine son-in-law to a man. Elizabeth agrees with me. But son, I wouldn't get any hopes up if I was you. Rebecca is only a little over fourteen and she has a long time ahead before she will be old enough to marry. Girls her age sometimes get their hearts and minds set on what they want for a future, taking advantage of present circumstances that do not materialize. If, by chance, the future does bring you two together in about three years, Elizabeth and I will be happy to have you as part of our family." Shaking his hand he told him, "I wish you Godspeed," turned and walked down the gangway.

Andy walked over to the railing and watched the wagon with the Ogdens and their baggage head up the dock toward Baltimore. He waved a lot of goodbye waves and saw Rebecca blowing him kisses just as she had when he was on watch in the crows nest. Tears started to well in his eyes until they flowed and he was crying. Then, he came to realize he had seen someone leave whom he loved.

With his personal belongings sitting on the dock and his need to go home, hitch up a horse and come back to get them, his composure returned quickly. He made a quick walk around the ship to say good bye. He looked into places where he might find crew members loitering. He found a few of the shipmates and instructors he had lived and worked with for more than two years. Mostly casual was the partings. Both Silas and Mac threw their arms around him, telling him he was a special sailor after a cruise on the Java Sea. He thanked them, inviting them to stop at the farm to see him whenever the ship docked in Baltimore.

Before walking down the gangway, he went to the Captain's office to say good bye to his uncle Fred and Lieutenant Brown. The Lieutenant had already departed. Captain Fred Murphy asked him to sit down and talk a few minutes before leaving.

Andy said, "I have to get a horse and wagon from the farm. I will talk for a while, as long as I can leave in a half hour."

"Andy I was somewhat reluctant in bringing you aboard this vessel because I didn't think you had it in you to become a good cabin boy and sailor. You surprised me completely. You turned into the best cabin boy I have ever had. Your choice and training of Juan is working out perfectly for me and the ship. I think I must owe you an apology for my doubts. I know I owe you many a Thank You, because you tried hard and you learned fast. I'll finish by saying, if you ever want to go to sea again, I'll make you my First Officer in the position Lt. Brown now holds."

"At present I know I want to be on the farm, with the family, working with the animals, and planning for a future. I enjoyed this voyage and made a lot of friends. I learned what a sailor's life is like and admire everyone who follows the sea for a livelihood. I appreciate all that has been said and your offers to me for the future. Now, I am going home."

Andy pushed his chair back, stood up and thrust his hand forward to shake hands. He said, "Uncle Fred, Captain Murphy Sir, I wish you and the Java Sea the best of everything for your future. Good Bye."

With his sea bag thrown over his shoulder, Andy walked up the gradual incline toward the farm. He noticed there were some new houses on the left side of the road. Almost at the top of the rise there had been a new road cut through the Murphy property toward Jacobsville. Whatever was on it was behind the hill and he couldn't see anything from the Annapolis Road. He trudged on and turned into the driveway as his mother was coming from the barn with a basket of eggs. She sat them down and came running toward him, throwing her arms around him and screaming, "Andy's home, Andy's home."

The back door banged open and his sister Emily came running to become the second one to welcome him home. Somewhat shy about it, she managed to give him a kiss, and say, "I love you big brother. Tell me all about being on the ship."

Melinda asked Emily to pick up the eggs. Looping her arm through his, she walked with him toward the back door with her head on his shoulder, an uncomfortable position for Andy, carrying his sea bag. Still, he was happy, he was home.

The first thing he noticed as he went into the kitchen was the sink and pump. The old wooden sink was gone. A new black, cast iron sink had replaced it. A cast iron pump with its long handle was attached to the end of the sink saving many trips to the well to draw water, pulled up by a rope attached to the handle of a bucket.

Andy asked, "Where is Maria?"

Before answering Melinda said, "We received only one letter from you in the past two years." She then asked, "Did you get any letters from any of us while you were gone?"

"Mail never caught up with any of us the whole two years," Andy answered. "The letter you received was probably one I mailed on a Nova Scotia whaler heading north. Mom, I knew you were thinking of me, there just isn't any mail."

"Back to Maria," Melinda said. "She married Ralph Gleason in the fall of the year you sailed. Your father divided up the land to give each of you children seven hundred acres of the original land grant. Maria and Ralph live on the northeast corner of the original thirty-five hundred acres. They built a nice cottage and big barn. They have a baby boy ten months old. He is a beautiful baby. We all love him. You will, too. We plan to divide the remaining fourteen hundred acres among grandchildren."

"Where is Jimmy Mixon?"

"He went back to sea about six months ago. There was a ship going to China and he took a job on it. He said he had never been in that part of the world. He was a big help to us until he got the itch to go back to sea. We all got along good."

"How long before Dad will be home from work?"

"It will be at least two hours."

"I might as well take a horse and wagon down to the ship. I need to pick up some things I left piled on the dock. Do you and Emily want to go along for the ride?"

"I will stay home and work on supper. I am sure Emily will want to go. She is doing homework from school this time of day."

As Andy and Emily headed down the Annapolis Road they met Ralph coming home from the shipyard. They talked briefly and he told them Maria would be happy Andy is home. At the dock, some of the crew were still around and they helped him load his things, making it a quick turn around for him.

Plodding along toward home, Daniel Murphy couldn't believe his ears as he heard someone say, "Want a ride, Dad." It sounded just like Andy. He turned his head and saw his own horse and wagon. He looked up to the driver, reached for a wheel to steady his balance and said, "Oh, thank God you're home son." Andy jumped down and gave him a big hug. There were tears of joy in the eyes of both father and son.

"I'm finished with going to sea. I plan to stay home and become a farmer. I'll work for you. As soon as I can I'll buy a piece of land to farm. Baltimore should be a good source of business for farm products."

"You already have a seven hundred acre farm from the land grant. A good farmer can make a living off that much land. You can use anything you want from the home farm. I think you'll do well, son. Ralph and Maria have been making money off their acreage and he's a ship builder. You're on the right track."

*   *   *   *

Andy got his first letter from Rebecca three weeks later. The letters came periodically for three years. He wrote an answer to each one. He wanted to go to Washington to see her. He had invested in livestock and chicken. They kept him tied to home.

Just after her eighteenth birthday, Rebecca Ogden came to the front door of the Murphy farm and when Melinda opened the door she said, "I'm Rebecca Ogden, I'm here to marry Andy Murphy."

"I'm Andy's mother. Does he know you plan to marry him?"

"Yes. I told him, as we sailed from England to Nova Scotia on his ship."

"Come in, dear. Andy should be coming in from the barn any moment."

As Andy came in the back door, Rebecca ran to him and threw herself into his arms. She smothered him with kisses and told him, "I'm old enough to marry you now."

He told her, "That's great, because I love you."

She blended in with the Murphy family and they were married a week later in a small church on the Annapolis Road. Their lives together were good. They built a home and raised five sons and two daughters. They were successful on the farm and both lived happily into their eighties. They are buried side by side in a small cemetery behind the church where they were married. Changing times surround their small gravesite with large modern homes scattered over the land they farmed.

Andy and Rebecca Murphy are representative of the early settlers and pioneers of our United States of America.
They are the BEDROCK of our land.

About the Author

Averyl O. Reed: Born 1922, Thomaston, Maine. He grew up as an era ended with old vessels rotting along the coast. He listened to stories of old sailors. At 84, he has written an entirely fictional Cabin Boy story for his grandchildren, from *Gramps*. Averyl graduated High School in 1940, served in Navy on Heavy Cruiser Baltimore in Pacific during WWII. He *knows* the feel of a rolling deck and weeks at sea.

978-0-595-40492-6
0-595-40492-8

3628494

Made in the USA